CHRISTOPHER J. STOCKWELL

Squatting in the Shadow of an Ant

Second edition

ISBN (paperback): 978-1-963805-16-1
ISBN (hardcover): 978-1-963805-17-8
ISBN (digital): 978-1-963805-16-1

Editing by Nicole Fegan
Editing by Laura Stockwell
Cover art by Muhammad Maysum

This book was professionally typeset on Reedsy.
Find out more at reedsy.com

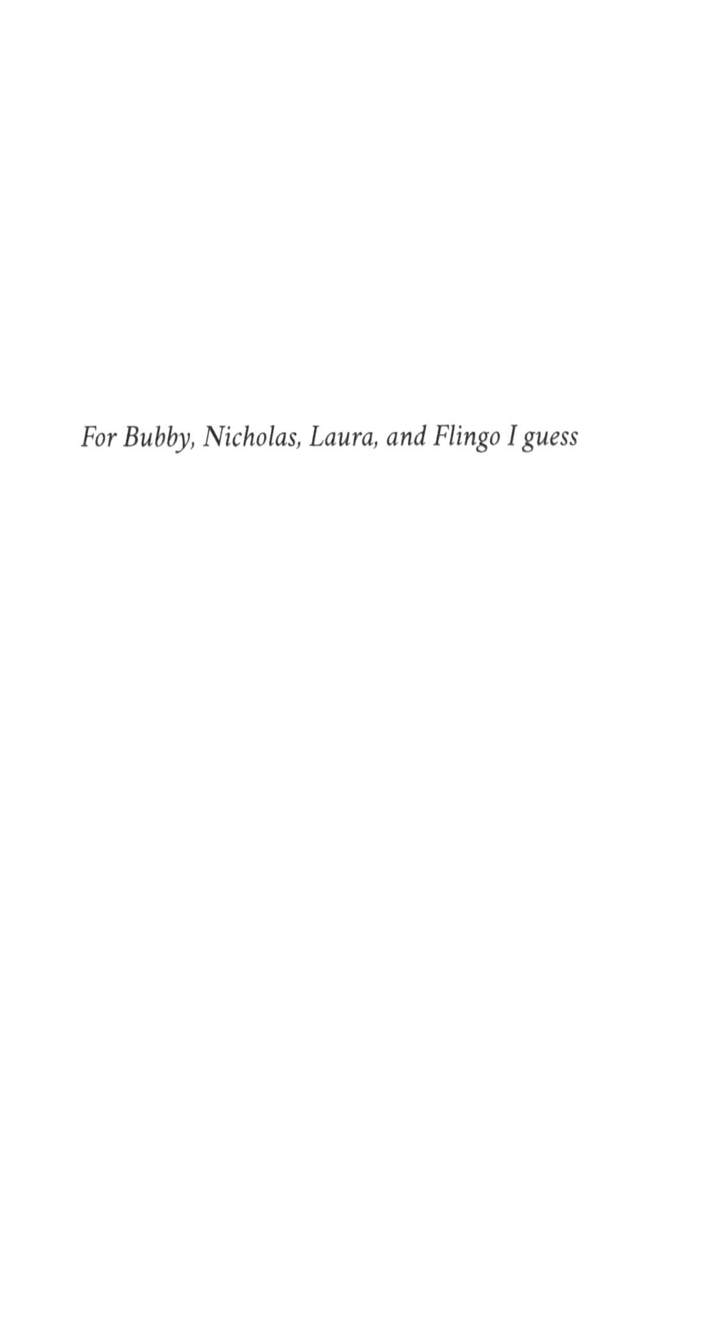
For Bubby, Nicholas, Laura, and Flingo I guess

It would have been so pointless
to kill himself that, even if he
had wanted to, the pointless-
ness would have made him un-
able.

— Franz Kafka, The Trial

Preface

"Why do you write?" She asked me during my first press interview for this book. "Why do you fuckin' care," is what my bestie Jack would say. He's always inside me trying to push his way out. When people take a tone, or give me orders, Jack bristles. Chris has a wife, kids, and a mortgage, so most of the time, Chris is charged with keeping Jack in check. Jack is why I write. The world moved on without Jack. His music scene is nothing but burnt ash from the campfire the night before. Jack's city doesn't exist anymore. It might as well be called Seattle 2.0.

I'm a lawyer, a prosecutor. When I put on a suit, you can't see me, or should I say you see my mask. Who am I? I'm the counterculture hiding in plain sight. Punk rock gave me a worldview, and I bring that worldview into society every time I speak in a courtroom or you flip the page of one of my books.

Why do I write, because after all these years, Jack and I are still pissed off at the world and everyone in it. And we've still got something to say about it.

Prologue

Was I speaking for Jack, or was Jack speaking for me? I'm the narrator, and while I do most of the speaking in this story, I never get an opportunity to really speak. Jack has got a lot to say, and most of it requires some high-brow interpretation from yours truly. The PNW hoi polloi vernacular takes a little gettin' used to, you know. Fortunately, I'm well versed. So well versed in fact, that it seems like Jack and I used to be the same person. If not the same, then nearly identical, and certainly inseparable.

At some point that changed. I'm not sure when, but it did. He went down the left fork, and I the right. Jack's story became more compelling as he became less salvageable. My story became less interesting as I became more capable. So I became the caretaker of Jack's story just as Beth became the caretaker of his mind. I hope I did it justice.

Chapter 1

J ack had gotten numb after that. He'd had to. He had surrendered himself to the Pierce County Sheriff's Department and was incarcerated at the Pierce County Jail for several weeks. Most of that time in county was a blur. Jack had attended several court hearings in his orange jumpsuit, where he had barely understood the proceedings. He had eaten food off a plastic tray. He had worn the county-issued slip-on shoes twenty-four hours a day because the concrete floor in his unit had been colder than an ice rink. He had asked for, and had never received, extra blankets, because those welded green steel bunks in his unit hadn't been much warmer than the floor.

To pass the time, Jack had read books and played cards with his cellmates, of which he'd had about sixty-three. Jack was guessing, but 4C had had sixteen bunk beds in the top cell, and it had had sixteen bunk beds in the bottom cell, and they had always seemed full. There had been movie nights, too, which Jack had loved whether he liked the movie or not. Breakfast had been at four in the morning, and lights out had been at ten, but other than the terrible hours, jail had sort of been like a non-stop slumber party for grown men with very little to no drugs or booze. Plus, the hours hadn't been too bad after all. Once you had eaten breakfast, you could just go back and sleep for a few more hours in your bunk. Nobody at county gave a shit if you were using your time productively.

Jack had preferred to sleep until lunch and then read after lights out by the halo of a streetlight that had shone through to his bunk. He'd had a top bunk, so it had been difficult for the corrections officers to tell what he was doing on their rounds, assuming they even cared. The windows had been that distorted shatter-proof glass they used, which made it impossible to see outside. The jail was in downtown Tacoma, and the windows had kept Jack, and everybody else, from seeing what was going on outside, but they hadn't filtered out the sounds of the city. Jack knew the corner of the city his cell had pointed out at. It had pointed toward Hilltop from 9th and Yakima. He had been able to hear people late on Friday and Saturday nights stumbling home from the bar, mentally ill homeless people screaming, fender benders, and more than a few fights.

The books had kept his mind mostly occupied, but in truth, Jack had looked forward to being transferred to a prison. Jail had been like drowning twenty yards from shore. Jack had been so close to where he wanted to be, but just hadn't been able to get there. Prison was like being stranded in a lifeboat in the middle of the ocean: no reason to struggle, just get comfortable and hope someone came along to rescue you at some point.

He had read three Stephen King novels while he sat in the county jail: *The Stand*, *The Shining*, and *Misery*. He had liked *The Stand* best, but had identified most with Paul Sheldon's plight in *Misery*. Halfway through *The Shining*, Jack had gotten a new bunkmate who didn't play cards, and by the time *The Stand* was finished, he'd accepted a plea bargain and was off to McNeil Island to do a stretch of three years and two months.

Three years was a long time, but it wasn't life. McNeil had been the last island prison operating in the United States when Jack was there. Walking off the prison bus down the catwalk at Steilacoom Dock had felt like living a Johnny Cash song. The feeling had faded by the time he was on the full little ferry to the island. By the time Jack had arrived, the old cell houses at McNeil had no longer been in operation. Instead, Jack had arrived at a nearly new facility. He had been told by the corrections officer escorting him across the water on the prison's ferry tug that the facility was dormitory style. Inside the processing center, Jack had seen pictures of the old cell house at McNeil, and it had given him the willies. It looked just like the rusty old cell house at another island prison in the middle of the San Francisco Bay: Alcatraz. Jack had visited it with his family when he was a kid, and he had never forgotten it. Mental institutions were not nice places, but those old cell houses looked like hen sheds, with rows of cages stacked on top of each other, wide open to the elements.

The new McNeil was more like Jack imagined reform school was like, and he had taken to it pretty quickly. The worst part, for him, had been the five-thirty wake up time. It hadn't been like county jail, either, where you just went back to sleep after breakfast. At McNeil, you ate breakfast, and then you went to your prison job, but even that had gotten to be routine after a couple of weeks.

Because McNeil housed only minimum and medium security prisoners, its air hadn't quite been ripe with the sheer terror that the constant threat of violence brought. Based on his offense, he knew he was lucky to have been classified as medium security, and lucky to have been sent to McNeil at all. Jack had been arrested dozens of times. He'd been committed several times. Fortunately for him, he hadn't been convicted of a crime until then. That was all that had kept him out of a maximum-security facility. He could have ended up someplace like Walla Walla where the threat of daily violence is a welcome reprieve from the reality of actual daily violence. That, and a tenacious public defender. His public defender had gone to Harvard Law School, and despite trying to hide it, was clearly from money. "His preppy ass was just out there slummin' it as a public defender in Tacoma for a couple years until he went and started his real life, probably at daddy's big Manhattan law firm." All this was grand, but to say that McNeil was violence-free, or that there hadn't been serious animosity and drama amongst the prisoner population would be erroneous. But again, McNeil had been more like *Reform School Girls*, less like *American Me.*

Jack had gotten a lot of visitors at first. You were actually allowed three visits per week, and McNeil was right outside Tacoma, so most people he knew had lived well within an hour's drive. After a while, they had tapered off. After a few months, it had mostly just been Beth and Jack's mom. Jack's mom had come once a month religiously, and Beth about every other weekend. Of course, he had been allowed to make phone calls, and he had talked to Beth a few times a week. That had held true for about a year, but eventually he had stopped calling

Beth altogether.

It hadn't been a principled stance on his part, or another guy on hers, not so far as Jack knew, anyway. One day, he had called and gotten her machine. He had gotten her machine at a time that she was always around. The next day had been Friday, and he hadn't called. She hadn't showed up during visiting hours Saturday, and then she hadn't showed up for visiting hours on Sunday. He had gotten her on the phone on Tuesday, and she said had she she had a present for him, and would bring it on Saturday.

That Saturday she had brought Jack a book called *You Can't Win*. It was the autobiography of a career criminal in the early twentieth century who had ultimately worked at a newspaper in San Francisco, lectured on prison reform, written his autobiography, and apparently committed suicide rather than become a burden on his friends. Beth had brought Jack a Bible of sorts for the down and out. The author's name was Jack, Jack Black. Jack admired Mr. Black, especially his conviction and character. Jack Black had had a code and stuck to it. Even his seeming choice to die on his own terms rather than become a burden on his friends had complied with that personal code. To some commentators, his ostensible suicide may have seemed self-righteous or selfish, or even the last attempt of an old man to garner attention, but not to Jack. Not at that point in his life.

Jack had spent all week reading and then rereading *You Can't Win*. Calling Beth hadn't occurred to him. Beth hadn't shown up on Saturday, and then she hadn't shown up on Sunday. That wasn't strange. She had been coming about once every other week, and she had just visited the week prior. She hadn't come that next weekend either, but Jack's mom had and as he'd requested, she had brought him a copy of *Junkie* by William S. Burroughs, which he was not obsessed with. Calling Beth hadn't seemed important. Understanding that there were other people like himself had. After two weeks without a call, Beth hadn't felt very important, and she had intended to tell him so when she came that weekend. The guard at the front office where visitors were allowed in, who openly disliked Jack and was secretly obsessed with Beth, had told her that Saturday that Jack hadn't wanted to see her.

It took about a month, but she had finally written Jack a letter. Beth had written that she still loved Jack, but that she was devastated by how he'd treated her. She, however, had made no reference to his refusal to see her that Saturday. Her intent had been reconciliation, and the continuation of their relationship as it had been. Jack had understood it as a request for separation from him, which had not shocked him, as he had severely neglected Beth over the past several weeks. After he had gotten her letter, he had called at a time he knew she'd be at work. He hadn't wanted to talk. He had wanted to leave a message. He hadn't. When her machine had come on, he had just hung the receiver up. They had not communicated again until some time after Jack's release from prison.

Jack had kept the letter on one of this two shelves in his cell. At McNeil, you had an actual room that was rarely locked down, and in it you and your cellmate had a bunk, a desk, and two shelves to keep personal items. Jack's bottom shelf had housed his clothes and toiletries. His top shelf had held his books, a couple photographs of Beth, and letters from his friends, mom, and Beth.

Jack's roommate had been a middle-aged black man named Frank. Frank had kept very few personal items on his shelves, just clothes, toiletries, a bible, and a book called *Alcoholics Anonymous*. Frank had had a medium-length, unkempt, salt-and-pepper afro and a powerful little frame. He couldn't have been more than five-foot-seven, but he had probably weighed in at two hundred pounds. On Jack's first day, Frank had told him, "I sleep on the bottom bunk, I always sleep on the bottom bunk, don't ask if we can switch. Ever!" Jack wasn't even sure Frank could have climbed the ladder to the top bunk. He had been about as wide as he was tall.

Frank had reminded Jack of one of those yellow barrels full of sand they put at freeway exits to absorb kinetic energy from crashing cars. They were actually called impact attenuators, and Frank had certainly been an impact attenuator. Hitting him could only realistically have resulted in you injuring yourself. A few months into Jack's sentence, he had been walking with his breakfast tray full of food when he had run into what appeared to be a ten-foot-tall Native American inmate. Jack had tried to apologize and hadn't noticed the giant's right fist was already in transit toward his face. Frank had magically appeared between Jack and the giant, harmlessly absorbing the punch on his ample shoulder while simultaneously defusing the situation.

Jack had only been a few months in when the mess hall incident with Running Cloud, the giant Native American, had happened. At the time, Jack hadn't understood how he had missed seeing Running Cloud's haymaker coming but Frank had known what was going to happen from across the mess hall. Jack had been a newb. After he'd been in for a while, Jack could see the Matrix, but at that time, Frank had been Morpheus, and Jack had just been Neo falling off a building.

Jack and Frank had both worked in the facilities department. Frank had been in the electrical shop, and Jack had been in the paint shop. They hadn't seen each other much during the day, but their unit had walked to the mess hall together for breakfast, and both their shops had been in the same building, so they had walked to work together. They had always seen each other at dinner, and sometimes, when their workdays had ended at the same time, they'd walked back to the unit together. Plus, they had shared a dorm room. "They don't call 'em cells in McNeil. It's like they want you to think it's college or some shit! When people ask me if I went to college, I tell 'em, yeah, I went to McNeil University, and I learned how to paint concrete prison walls." Frank had gone to church on Sunday mornings, and Alcoholics Anonymous meetings on Tuesday and Thursday evenings, neither of which Jack had attended. "I didn't go to no AA meetin' at first, but I did start readin' that Big Book of his when he wasn't around. Fuck the church, though! I never fuckin' went there!"

Jack didn't really think there was a solution in the book, and he certainly hadn't understood how it worked, but he had liked the stories a lot, and eventually he had started going to the AA meetings with Frank. The first meeting Jack had gone to was the Tuesday night meeting. It had been called "Free as a Jailbird Now." AA meetings always had ironic names that were supposed to be funny, and most of them just sounded like some bad dad joke. "That said, Lynyrd Skynyrd was pretty fuckin' cool for seventies rock." The meetings had been held in the prison. Frank hadn't told Jack that he was the secretary of the Tuesday night meeting. Frank also hadn't told Jack that he was going to be the speaker at his first meeting until he announced it in the meeting ten seconds before Jack was supposed to speak. Frank had also become Jack's AA sponsor, a fact that Frank had only informed Jack of after the meeting.

Frank had been convicted of a vehicular homicide. He had been in a blackout when it happened. He had woken up in the King County Jail and had never been home since. He'd done nearly seven years of a ten-year sentence, which on its face seemed unfair, because Jack's homicide had happened in a blackout and he had only received three years and a couple of months. Plus, Jack's sentence had already been reduced several weeks for time served in county, and he assumed he would get out early for good behavior. To Jack, it had seemed like either his sentence was too easy, or Frank's was too harsh. Neither conclusion had sat right with him.

Nothing said is meant to minimize that Frank was an alcoholic, or that he'd ended somebody's life with an automobile, but he hadn't been a lifelong criminal, either. He had worked in the electric shop at McNeil because he had been a commercial electrician before he came to McNeil. He had been thirty-nine years old when he was sentenced, and his vehicular homicide conviction had been a first offense. He had a son and daughter that had been teenagers when he went in. They were grown by then, and they had visited sometimes. His son had actually gotten married and had a daughter of his own. Frank had a wife too, but she had divorced him a couple years into his sentence.

Frank hadn't kept pictures or any personal belongings from his life because his life no longer existed. He had been denied bail pending trial. He was never allowed to go back to his life after that blackout, not even to put his affairs in order. His family had become different people. His wife had remarried, and the kids he was raising had become adults with lives of their own. The house he had raised those kids in had been sold by his ex-wife and was somebody else's home. The kids' lunchboxes on the counter and coats thrown haphazardly on the floor of the closet had only been seven years ago, but that life could never exist again. Being reminded he had missed the last few years of it had been too much for Frank. Alcoholism had robbed him of his life, and it robbed his family of its father.

Frank had gotten out about a year before Jack, having done about eight years of a ten-year sentence. Jack did just over two for essentially the same offense. At the end of the day, in Frank, society had lost a contributing member, capable of rehabilitation for the better part of a decade. Simultaneously, in Jack, society had returned a hopelessly broken cog back to the streets in just over two years. Jack lacked the vocabulary and education to articulate the situation in academic terms, but based on his experiences at McNeil, he clearly understood the implications of what we now call institutional racism and white privilege. "In other words, it was pretty fucked up!"

For a while after Frank was gone, and Beth hadn't come around anymore, Jack had mostly served his sentence in his head. By that time, it seemed that visitors had started coming around again. The members of the original crew had showed up sporadically, but often. One member of the original crew, at that time, was about to serve a sentence of his own at McNeil.

Jack's mom had showed up like clockwork once a month: second Saturday, two in the afternoon. Jack assumed her visiting time had been a well-grooved habit. She had been used to supporting Jack financially, and the second Saturday was the day after her first payday of the month. She had always put money on his commissary account and brought him whatever book he'd been asking for and some takeout food for them to eat for lunch. She picked her first payday for a reason. She'd put money on Jack's commissary account even if she needed it for rent, so she had come the day after her first payday of the month, well before the next month's rent was due.

Other than that, he had done his best to isolate himself from the outside world completely, but engaged pretty heavily within the prison itself. The Frank Model, he called it. During that time, he'd actually started serving as secretary of the Tuesday AA meeting at McNeil. Running Cloud had been the secretary of the Thursday meeting at the same time as Jack was secretary for Tuesday.

Also, during that time, Jack had read *Ham on Rye* by Charles Bukowski. The prison counselor had suggested he read *Catcher in the Rye* by J.D. Salinger. Somehow, Jack's mom had turned up with *Ham on Rye* instead. "That turned out to be a blessin' in disguise. I read *Catcher in the Rye* after *Ham on Rye*. It was about some rich kid who keeps getting' expelled from prep schools. I mean, it's probably a pretty good book if you're a rebellious teenager in Chappaqua, but it didn't do shit for me. Bukowski is all about LA, skid row, old man hotels, dive bars full of alcoholics. He speaks my language." *Catcher in the Rye* was the first and last Salinger book Jack ever read, but he had spent the remainder of his sentence reading everything Charles Bukowski ever wrote.

The books Jack had read in there were timeless. They hadn't existed in his time. They hadn't even existed in their own time. Philosophers and craftsmen of great fiction rarely used their surroundings or time to make their works interesting. They used their unique minds and experiences to drive their writing. A spattering of worldly reference here and there, maybe, but just for flavor, the way a great chef sparingly sprinkles spices to create something pleasing to the palette. Other than punk rock music, it was the only true art and culture Jack had ever absorbed. Jack's mom had brought at least one book a month, but Jack had read one or two books a week. The library at McNeil had filled that donut hole. It hadn't had anything very current or provocative, but it had been chock-full of classics, so Jack had read a lot of Hemingway, Melville, and Kafka, each of which had offered different and interesting merits.

Other than that, time had mostly just rolled by just like it always did. People say doing time, and that's exactly what it was. There was no vacation to look forward to. There was no big date on Saturday night. Just one day after another. After a while, Jack hadn't even counted days, or even months. He hadn't even meant to stop counting. It had just happened. One day he had been in the yard during rec time and he wished he'd brought his jacket. That had been it, no jacket. Right then, he had realized it was the middle of November. The last time he'd thought about what time of the year it was, it had been August. He hadn't thought about the days or even the weeks, not in terms of his sentence, anyway. AA had been on Tuesday and Thursday, he had worked Monday through Saturday, and his mom had showed up on Saturdays, but only once a month. That said, other than a vague cognizance of a couple days of the week, he hadn't really given his sentence much thought, not in a long time.

As he had walked the fence line in the yard that November morning, he'd had to really think about how much time he had left. "There was no way to know for sure. Shit like time off for good behavior—whatever the fuck that meant—made it hard to work out, but at that time, I think I'd done about fourteen months." Jack *had* gotten time off for good behavior: two and a half months. How does someone with six physical altercations, two with corrections officers, and no less than twenty contraband violations get credited time off for good behavior? "It's because mostly everybody else in there was a bigger fuck up than I was, so I looked well-behaved by comparison." Even Jack had understood that "good behavior" in prison didn't even rise to the level of acceptable behavior in the rest of society.

For Jack, prison had been boot camp, an orientation to life mostly free of substances and that ever-steady drum beat of mental illness. There had been too much structure and not enough time for his mental illnesses to severely torment him. Every day, he had known exactly where and when he was going to be waking up, when he was going to sleep at night, and at what time meals would be. And, thanks to the meal calendar in the mess hall, Jack had even known what he'd be eating at every meal for the remainder of the month. His OCD had loved the perfection of the meal calendar, but had also caused terror and trauma in him when the kitchen unexpectedly changed the meal plan, which had happened with all too much frequency.

After Frank left, Jack had bunked with nobody in particular, even though it was someone very specific. He name was Barry, but he was so uninteresting that Jack had referred to him as nobody in particular as though it was his name. "Who is your new cellmate?" Jack's mom had asked at a visiting hour. "No fuckin' body in particular," Jack had responded.

Jack had taken pride in his immaculate cell and his new muscles, courtesy of the gym equipment in the yard, that swelled the way water balloons did when you attached them to a garden hose. When he flexed, they had bulged the way those same water balloons did when you squeeze them. Jack's mind had woken up, and it had jackhammered routes through sludge that had been blocking pathways that had never properly developed. Where no roadways existed, his mind had built them. If Jack had spent another twenty years at McNeil, he could have truly made something out of his life. Or, at least, he could have had some serenity and peace in his mind, a steep price to pay for mental wellness.

That's not to say that Jack's alcoholism, drug addiction, and mental illnesses hadn't continued to plague him to some extent. There had been drugs and alcohol at McNeil, but they had been hard to get, and there had been no steady supply of either. Jack drank exactly five times in prison, and not once had he been able to acquire enough hooch to get properly drunk. The drugs that had been available were, again, only available in limited quantities. "What's a balloon of coke going to do except make one afternoon of work fly by. It's like gettin' a six pack of beer, you can't get drunk, you can't even barely get a buzz off six. This one guy would give you a balloon for a list of commissary items that was 'bout a hundred fuckin' bucks, why fuckin' bother at those prices, right." Without enough booze or drugs to get properly high or drunk, he had lost interest in even trying to get fucked up.

For several months after he arrived, his PTSD, OCD, depression, anxiety, borderline schizophrenia, and bipolar disorder had kept him climbing the walls, scared of every sideways glance another inmate threw his way, but eventually he had got the hang of being in prison without prescription medications, illicit drugs, or even his undisputed bestie, alcohol.

Jack's overwhelming life problems had been pushed into the background, and his focus had shifted to what was directly in front of him. In much the same way that a man stranded on a deserted island ceased to worry about his rent and instead became interested in how to kill a small animal for his next meal, things like not being stabbed with a fork in the mess hall had become imperative. All those things that were very bothersome in the real world had seemed to be of little consequence in McNeil. Surviving his sentence, both mentally and physically, had become the big thing in his life. At McNeil, the equivalent of no money for rent had been avoiding a beating during rec time, or filling seventeen hours a day without going crazy.

Chapter 2

Anything you do for long enough becomes normal. It's called habituation. One year was all it took for Jack to become totally habituated into prison life. For Jack, one solid year of doing the same thing day in and day out was quite an achievement, even if he'd had little choice in the matter, but doing it without prescription medication, drugs, or alcohol was unprecedented. That whole time had been spent just figuring out how to get by in there. When Jack looked back on it, he imagined what it would have been like if he hadn't met Frank. Then his mind would immediately begin creating every worst-case scenario. To him, the thought of the first year at McNeil without Frank was too scary to think about, but once that trap in his obsessive mind was sprung, it would usually cause hours, if not days, of rumination on those could-have-been-terrible outcomes.

Several months after Frank was released, Ron had arrived on his unit. The abandoned house had really been abandoned then. Todd and Ron had finally gotten pinched. The house had been raided after an extensive sting operation. Ron had taken a plea bargain and gotten eighteen months at McNeil. Todd had refused a deal and was convicted at trial. He'd gotten two and a half years at Monroe. It was likely the first and only time Todd hadn't chosen the path of least resistance. He had chosen poorly and did more time in a harder prison for his poor choice.

Ron had been a perfect fit for prison. He was industrious and motivated. His life, from a very early age, had consisted of scheming to improve his lot in life. His goal over every summer break when they were kids had been to trade or sell enough of his old beat-up, worn-out shit to get new shit for the next school year. When he fell short of the mark, he had resorted to stealing shit he could sell like bikes and car stereos. If he still hadn't had what he wanted for school by late August, he had just started going to the shops at the mall and taking what he wanted. His method had been to just put on whatever clothes he wanted, snip the security tag, and walk out. When someone figured out what he was doing, he had run.

Ron had done pretty well at this, too, much better than his siblings. Food had been a luxury around their house, while drugs were abundant. Sometimes, he'd just sold the weed and pills he had stolen from his mom. Sometimes, when she ran out of weed and pills, he'd sold her cheap wine and cigarettes. There had always been kids in the neighborhood in the market for Ron's mom's drugs, cigs, and hooch. Ron had lived and died by his wits. He was the first kid that Jack had personally known who came from a truly broken home.

He had run away from home dozens of times, beginning when he was fourteen. When he was lucky, he had lived with one of three older siblings. When he wasn't lucky, he had slept in an abandoned car, newspaper bin, or even his own backyard. There had been an old pickup truck canopy by the detached garage back there. All told, between the ages of fourteen to eighteen, he had probably spent seven or eight months sleeping under that canopy without his mom ever suspecting he was there.

Even in the midst of all this confusion, Ron had been able to graduate from high school. Jack had never understood why he bothered. It wasn't as though Ron had showed any interest in going to college. Jack had come by that canopy to find Ron under it in his sleeping bag, reading textbooks with a flashlight. Apparently, doing schoolwork had been a great time killer and distraction from the rest of his life. Also, he may not have intended to go to college, but he had figured that a high school diploma would secure him at least enough of an education to get some semi-skilled blue-collar job. Since getting away from his mom's house had been his primary purpose in life, finishing high school had seemed like the most expedient way to move away from there and not return.

Through scheming, Ron had survived, and that hadn't changed because he was locked down in a prison. If anything, prison made Ron even more crafty than he had been when he went in.

Chapter 3

During the last six months of his sentence, Jack had started to loosen up and even enjoy his life. Ron had worked in the paint shop with him during the day. It was the most time they'd spent together since they were in junior high school.

Ron had become a reliable merchant of contraband items. He'd sold drugs. His drug mules had mostly been the teenagers that dealt for him on the outside. When it came to drugs in prison, the smaller the better. Also, things that could be snorted or swallowed had been preferred. It made sense. Sneaking in an ounce of weed would have been hard. It was big, and it smelled, and people had mainly wanted to smoke it. Nothing about any of that had been fine-tuned for prison. Coke, meth, and pills had been the bulk of the trade in there.

Other than occasionally holding some of Ron's stash, Jack had avoided the contraband trade. Ron had offered to cut him in numerous times, and of course had offered him free drugs often. For the first, and only, time in Jack's life, he had avoided substances. He had kept going to the AA meetings. He had actually enjoyed them by that point. Jack had always shared in meetings and had normally held a service position. Ron had attended, too, but mostly because it was the best place at McNeil to deal drugs.

For some time, Jack had been trying to keep the outside world from coming into McNeil, and he had become quite comfortable in his isolation. Ron's arrival had brought his old life right into the prison walls. Two years earlier, that might have been a problem for Jack. He'd been quite successful at adopting the "Frank Method" of doing time. That is, keep your outside life on the outside, and keep your inside life on the inside. It had served its purpose well. It had gotten Jack through his sentence, but things had changed. Frank had no longer been around to give him advice. Even if he had been there, he'd only been out a short time anyway, so what could Frank tell him about the outside. He likely had forgotten how to be on the outside himself. Jack just hoped he hadn't carved "Frank was here" into a halfway house wall. In a short time, Jack would, once again, be on his own, without a guide.

Between Ron's presence and the handful of months remaining on his sentence, Jack had felt like the prison was melting away right in front of him.

There were times where he had doubted anyone would even stop him if he'd decided to just walk out of the prison down to the dock and catch the ferry back to the mainland. The prison counselor had met with him often about his reintegration plan. These meetings had terrified Jack. Jack would be free to go when his sentence was served, but there were resources for him to utilize if he so chose. There were halfway houses, lists of employers that hired ex-convicts, etc.

During one of those meetings, it had occurred to Jack that, thanks to his newly acquired prison muscles, he could snap that prison counselor's neck before anyone in the office complex could stop him. Then, they would have had to keep him in prison. It had been a comforting thought for a minute. Then it had been an intrusive and scary obsessive thought. He would have been in prison for years to come, that much was true. But he would certainly not have stayed at McNeil. Jack would have been relocated to some terrible maximum-security prison somewhere in the state, probably Walla Walla. Twenty or thirty years locked down twenty-three hours a day with the most violent criminals in the state was not what Jack had in mind. Right then, Jack had decided to accept that he would once again be a free man.

Chapter 4

As expected, when the day had come to actually go home, Jack was ambivalent about it. Jack assumed he must have become institutionalized quicker than anyone in history. In just over two years, he'd become reliant on prison life, so much so that, for several months leading up to his release, the thought of leaving had given him awful panic attacks. In the past, being released from confinement had always been an occasion to celebrate with debauchery. This had not been like those other times. Jack had thought about all the hard days he'd lived in his life, and how, late into any given hard day, he had inevitably thought to himself that if he'd known what the day had in store for him when he'd woken up, he would have just stayed in bed. He had figured his whole life was about to become one long, never-ending hard day, and there would be no bed to hide in.

At the same time, it had been impossible to ignore that he was literally being released from prison. Even if he crashed and burned in spectacular fashion, he'd been away for so long that, for a while, everything would seem new again. His mom had been scheduled to meet him at the ferry dock on the mainland. The ferry was underway, and that boat rocking back and forth under his feet had felt strange. Seeing his mom hadn't seemed so weird. He'd seen her dozens of times while he was at McNeil. But the gravel under his feet on the walk from the ferry dock to the car had felt alien.

Jack had been twenty-two. He was a killer, and an ex-convict. He had been going home to live with his mommy. Jack's ability to process stimuli had been overloaded. He hadn't even started drinking right away. Nor had he found drugs, fast girls, or trouble of any kind. Just processing his situation had left him exhausted. He'd felt high, but not the good kind of high. He'd felt too high, crazy high. He'd slept a minimum of twelve hours a day for the next week. Most of the time he had been awake, but he had stayed in his bed pretending to sleep so his mom wouldn't try talking to him.

After his mom went to bed, he'd gotten up to watch TV and try to eat. He had mostly eaten Ritz crackers with little slices of cheddar cheese on them. He'd had a glass of milk to wash them down, but that had only been on "good" days. Many days, he had eaten nothing at all. Eating had been something that he could control, and he had realized that after sixteen or seventeen hours of fasting he stopped being hungry altogether. He hadn't even controlled sleep. He could lie in bed all day long, but he hadn't been able to control whether he actually fell asleep. Whether he ate or not was completely within his control, and he had clung to that sliver of control because there had been no other ropes to cling to.

Unfortunately, that control had eventually become the basis of a new addiction and led to more lack of control. "I know, an anorexic dude! It's a little lame, but it totally happened." In combination with the general appetite-suppressing effects of the drugs he had routinely used and the alcohol he had consumed, not eating became a problem that would plague him for the remainder of his life.

Eventually, Jack had risen from his bed and joined the living. The novelty of the world outside McNeil had worn off, and he had been hungry for booze, ass, and dope. Happiness was trying to simultaneously satisfy as many of your physical, and mental cravings as humanly possible. That had been Jack's motto for as long as he could remember.

It wasn't that he had woken up, because he hadn't really been asleep. Two years at McNeil had made him forget what it felt like to come out of a blackout suddenly.

His head had been hyper-extended over the headrest of the passenger's seat of his mom's car. Jack's dad had never come to visit him in prison, so he had figured asking him to borrow his truck was a non-starter. His mom, on the other hand, had been more than happy to offer up her car keys even though Jack didn't have a valid license. "I'm back on the streets behind the wheel, the paper's gone but I still got the feel." As he'd sat, half-conscious, taking sips of a warm 40oz of malt liquor, he had caught a glimpse of himself in the rearview mirror and realized there was a rolled-up dollar bill sticking out of one of his nostrils. He hadn't been able to remember snorting any meth that night, but, seeing the dollar bill jammed up his nose, he had figured the meth he didn't remember snorting had been the only thing keeping him awake. He had peeked inside the little hole at the top of the 40oz bottle for a minute, but it had given him vertigo.

The girl blowing him hadn't realized, or hadn't cared, that Jack had whiskey dick. He hadn't recognized the top of her head, but he had recognized the parking lot of the roofing company he had been parked in. It was on South Tacoma Way, and he had inferred that the unrecognized bobbing head was a prostitute he had picked up in his blackout. Jack had immediately started hoping that the bill rolled up in his nose was a twenty. He had assumed the hundred bucks his mom had given him earlier was long gone, and he had been right. "That was a one-dollar bill crammed up my nose, not a twenty. That was one angry prostitute. She punched my cock so fuckin' hard when she realized I couldn't pay her, but I had the whiskey dick, so I didn't really feel it. She should have punched for my fuckin' balls."

Jack was back, but Jack's motto had been broken. He suspected his motto had never worked that well in the first place. Sometimes, he felt like debauchery had kept him from sinking lower into the abyss of his soul, but when he was honest with himself, he knew it had just distracted him from a sinking that never really abated. There was no happiness, not in the bottle, not in that line, certainly not in the angry prostitute's warm mouth, and definitely not in his own existence. "I don't think happiness is really a thing. It's like God. People made up God because they're afraid of not existin', and to people, existin' is all. People made up happiness because they can't deal with sadness, and to people, lack of sadness is all. That's all there is to it."

And what exactly had he done two years for? Jack had never thought about it in prison, but after his release, it had come back to him a lot. He hadn't meant to kill that biker. The way Jack figured it, that guy hadn't really left him any choice. That hadn't made it righteous, but it had made it self-defense. He believed he had done time for a killing that a prosecutor wouldn't even have charged him for if he had been someone with status, money, or a decent defense lawyer. Worst of all, it had been a disagreement over half a gram of crank; that was it. Just a couple of sped-up, drunk dopers arguing over a little bit of meth. That biker had tried to screw Jack, that was true. Jack had felt blood rush to his face, and his hands had started trembling. He knew he should have forgotten it. He knew that had been the moment to walk out. But he hadn't been able to. Jack had showed that biker the handle of his PPK. In return, that biker had swung the heavy end of the axe handle he had kept under the kitchen table at Jack's head.

In her police statement, the biker's girlfriend had stated that if Jack had left then, that would have been the end of it. Instead, Jack had smashed a half-full 40oz bottle into the biker's skull. The glass had shattered and the skull had popped simultaneously, and when it had, it made a mostly indescribable disgusting wet noise. Not that Jack remembered, but the girlfriend's statement had been graphic. She had run away. She had gotten in her car and gone to her sister's house for the night. That dope fiend biker had collapsed right there in his kitchen nook. Jack had done like any smart addict; he had kept his money, grabbed that biker's meth, and hit the road. The driveway was as far as he had made it before he had blacked out and then proceeded to pass out in his car. By the time the girlfriend came home the next day, it had been much too late for that biker.

The bottle being half full had made a significant impact. It had been like a hitter warming up with weights on his bat. The beer in the 40oz bottle had increased the velocity and impact of the bottle when it had hit his skull. It had shattered his temple, and the resulting sub-cranial bleeding had done him in while he lay there alone for the next twelve or so hours.

That was it; that was the story. It had cost him years of his life, this one moment of self-justified rage. He couldn't remember much of it, not when it happened, and honestly not years later, either. His brain had, over the years, filled in the gaps to construct a fairly likely chronology of events. This was based mostly on what the girlfriend had said in her statement, and the little Jack himself recollected.

He had stared across the parking lot at that dick-punching hooker sauntering away and decided to run her down. He had revved the engine up and dropped it into drive. The look on her face as his mom's shabby Corolla had begun to bear down on her had actually broken his tunnel vision for an instant.

That biker, Jim, hadn't really been a bad guy, and neither had his girlfriend. Her name was Stacy. Jack had actually spent quite a bit of time at that trailer talking to both of them when he was buying meth. Jim had been as fucked up that night as Jack had, and Jim had made a mistake in trying to cheat Jack, but Jack had made a worse mistake by not walking away. Now Jim was dead. Jim wasn't coming back, no matter what. Death was final.

Jack had veered the Corolla hard to the right and onto South Tacoma Way. He had missed that hooker by a couple of feet. It had felt like a couple of inches. Jack hadn't learned much in his life, but for at least one moment that night, another person's life had been more important to him than his pride. "And that's not nothin'!"

Chapter 5

G oing to prison had begun with a going-away party, so a welcome-home party had seemed like an appropriate way to bookend that chapter of Jack's life. The timing had been a little off, since Jack had been released almost two months earlier. There had, of course, been a coming-home dinner hosted by Jack's mom and grudgingly attended by his brother and father. That had been the day after he was released. A coming-home dinner with the family a couple of months prior was a far cry from what had been planned at Mike's house that night.

Lots of people used drugs that made them feel good. Shit like molly, shrooms, or acid. Jack was from Tacoma, and he liked his drugs dirty, not designer. Meth and PCP didn't feel good. They felt like a flesh-mutilating nightmare that you couldn't wake up from. Alcohol was no better. As a matter of fact, it was poison to the human body. Disorientation and vomit were the first side effects of alcohol. Complete blackouts, loss of consciousness, and a depressed nervous system came next. Keep drinking, and death was the final side effect. Death from alcohol could happen just like that from one night of drinking, but if it didn't get you like that, eventually it would get you with Cirrhosis. Jack felt that bottles of booze should have Mr. Yuck stickers on them just like the cleaning products under the sink did. Even though Jack drank every day, he still suffered from crippling hangovers. At many points, and for extended periods of time, Jack's life was really just a hangover spilling over into drunkenness, and then back into a hangover.

What a body will endure is quite amazing. What it will endure and keep functioning through is even more amazing. Sitting with his family during his welcome home dinner had felt nice, for once. Laurence hadn't been a bastard, and Jack's father hadn't been completely cold. They had sat in a wood-paneled booth overlooking Commencement Bay. As usual, Jack's mom had sat next to him, her on the aisle and Jack against the window. She had always sat next to him like that. He wondered if she had realized she was literally shielding him with her body. She had sat as a physical blockade, like she could keep the world from getting to him if she put herself in the way. Laurence and his father had sat next to each other stoically on the opposite side of the booth.

His mom, naïve as usual, had been hopeful. This was regrettable—not because of her hopefulness for her beloved son, but because she'd already lost the debate about what he'd do with his life. This was the case despite the fact that the discussion had not even taken place. Everybody had just known. Jack loved her for having faith in him, even to the last, and he felt guilt over what he continually put her through, but the pity he had for her was the strongest emotion of all. He could feel all the guilt in the world, but at the end of the day, when he looked at her, he felt pity. She was hopelessly deluded about Jack. All she saw was the sweet kid she'd raised. She refused to see, or wasn't capable of seeing, the lout he'd become.

Jack thought a lot about that family dinner on the night of his party at Mike's house. Mike's house hadn't really been a house so much as a studio apartment downtown. After him and his last girlfriend had broken up, he'd downsized considerably. That place had been similar in many ways to the studio apartments Jack and his friends had found themselves inhabiting at various points over the course of their lives. Similarly, Mike's building had been exactly the type of place you liked to party at, or live at for two months before being evicted. Mike had been there about a year.

It had mostly been filled with residents that

couldn't live anywhere else, and the pores of the building had reeked from depravity of every persuasion. Four stories of the biggest losers, prostitutes, crack dealers, speed dealers, fienders, beggars, punkers, stoners, actually crazy people, sort of crazy people, criminally insane people, criminally cutthroat people who were surprisingly sane, and any other square peg that the dirty little city had failed to jam into a round hole. On any given night, half the apartments in the building had been having a raucous party. The other half had just had a few friends over to smoke some rocks.

The building had been dangerous during its calmest moments, but after the sun went down, it had become downright terrifying. The bare brick walls on the inside had oozed anxiety and tension. There hadn't even been carpet in the hallways, just concrete floors, like the ones at McNeil. Jack had just done two years in prison, and walking into Mike's building had been more terrifying that anything he could remember ever doing. At least in prison, the corrections officers had broken up fights eventually. "At Mike's buildin', nobody was likely to break up shit." You could die in that building, and Jack found out later that the building had actually averaged about one homicide a month. At that building, the police hadn't shown up unless there was a body.

The fact that nothing short of a corpse ever brought out law enforcement meant it was equally unsurprising that the fire marshal never showed up to issue citations for fire code violations, either. On the night of the party, there had been no less than thirty people, many of them Jack and Mike's friends, literally crammed into Mike studio apartment like sardines. For the first time ever, Jack had noticed the fascinating aroma that three people's breaths made when you smelled them simultaneously. He had also realized that not only would he not be able to sit down at his own party, but even getting a beer seemed out of reach from where Jack was standing.

The people at the party had mostly been people that Jack knew—at least, they had been at ten o'clock. The faces had been just like the ones at the abandoned house the night Jack had killed Jim the biker. Other than Mike, they had consisted of a few people Jack would have called friends, a bunch he would have called acquaintances, and a handful that he either hadn't known, or hadn't cared for at all. "Today they call those ones you don't really like but are nice to nonetheless frenemies. By midnight, most of the friendly faces had cleared out, even the frenemies. They'd been replaced by the faces of people Jack had assumed just roamed from apartment to apartment in search of a free high.

Mike's big, round, vacant eyes had stared out

from the chair where he was sitting. Other than the stained and sheetless twin mattress on the floor, Mike's chair had been the only place to sit in the entire apartment. Jack hadn't noticed it before, but the more he had looked around, the more he had started to realize that Mike's apartment actually resembled a crack den. Normally, by midnight, Jack would have been well into a blackout, but he'd been smoking meth with this guy Brett earlier, so he had been quite aware of his surroundings. The meth always kept the blackout from happening, at least for a couple of hours. Jack wasn't addicted to meth, but it was always around, and he had infrequently smoked and snorted it order to keep the party going.

Jack didn't like crack and had only smoked it a handful of times. Tacoma was on the back end of its part in the crack epidemic of the eighties. Tacoma's part in that epidemic had been a significant one. Despite the epidemic being mostly in the rearview, it had still been pretty prevalent in Tacoma in the nineties. Most drugs hadn't scared Jack, but crack did. The few times he'd smoked it, he had immediately felt a sort of euphoria that made every problem in the universe so small it could fit on the head of a pin. Those problems had become so miniscule, one could say they just simply hadn't mattered. Of course, there was one problem that crack didn't make smaller; in fact, crack made this problem gigantic. That problem was, how does one get more crack?

The last time Jack had seen Mike had probably been a year previous, during visiting hours at Mc-Neil. That was before Mike and his last girlfriend had split. At that time, Mike still had his normal, husky build. He wasn't tall, but he normally carried a little extra weight. His cheeks had that cherub appearance, and his features were full. That night at the party, Jack hadn't really looked at Mike, until he had. Mike had been sitting in his chair, literally staring at the wall. There hadn't even been a TV in his place anymore. All his records had been gone. Jack hadn't even thought he had any clothes in the apartment, except what he was wearing, and what he was wearing was pretty drab. He'd had on two different shoes, filthy sweatpants, and an undershirt that had been white at one time. His eyes had been sunken and dark, and Jack estimated he had weighed no more than one hundred twenty-five pounds. He hadn't shaved in days, maybe weeks, and his hair had been thin and wiry.

Mike's crack-smoking "friends" had continued to crowd in, which had made Jack want to slip out. Jack had squeezed through the crowd to Mike. He'd had a glass pipe in his hand. Jack had hugged Mike and said he needed to get some air, and that he'd catch up with him later.

Jack had taken the stairs up to the roof. From the ledge facing straight west, Jack had been able to see the heart of downtown. If you looked straight east, you could see crack dealers at the Lucky 7 and the entrance to People's Park on 9th and MLK. Jack hadn't realized it at that moment, but four months later, Mike would be shot to death on that corner. Sickly, slender, and hollow, sitting in his chair, was how Jack had last seen Mike alive. Pale, puffy, and waxy, lying in his coffin, was how Jack had last seen Mike dead. Todd and Ron had still been locked up when it happened, so the mourners had consisted mostly of Jack, Mike's parents, and Mike's little brother. There had been ten times as many people crammed into his little apartment the night of Jack's party, none of whom had seen fit to show up at his funeral.

Jack had hopped into his mom's Corolla and headed up to the Lucky 7. The outside window ledge had been decorated with bottles of Cisco and King Cobra. Jack couldn't understand why someone would drink King Cobra on purpose. "For a quarter more you could get a bottle of Olde English. Why bother with that other garbage?" The guy at the cash register hadn't seemed to care who bought booze or cigarettes as long as they had money. Everybody in line had bought beer, and nobody had gotten carded. Jack hadn't even had a valid I.D. His driver's license had expired while he was in prison, and he hadn't bothered to get it renewed. It had made sense to Jack. When your parking lot was the biggest open-air crack market until Oakland, the cops weren't worried about teenagers getting wasted on beers.

Right before Jack had headed up to the roof, Mike had offered him the glass pipe, one big rock sitting in the blackened bowl. Jack had declined. Mike had said: "Suit yourself man, you've already experienced everythin'. You're not missin' anythin' at this point. You're just relivin' it. Most people don't even get to try it all once, much less live long enough to abuse it until it's borin'." The best Jack could do was to keep writing the same chapter over and over again. Best-case scenario, it would continue to be fun; worst-case, it would get harder and harder. The past few years had not been fun, and Jack had thought he could see which way the wind was blowing. That was the last thing Mike had ever said to Jack, and it had stuck to him like gum on the sole of your Vans.

Mike's crack problem hadn't magically trans-formed Jack into a choir boy, and the night had still been relatively young. Nobody had hassled him at the Lucky 7, which was a change of pace. Usually, he would have been offered crack by at least two dealers before he even had gotten in the door. He had gotten two forties of Olde English, bought two packs of Marlboro Reds, and filled the Corolla's gas tank. He had cracked the first 40oz. It had been cold going down his throat. He had enjoyed it because those forties only stayed cold for about two minutes, tops. He had reached into his pocket for a smoke and found a quarter of crank he'd bought from that guy Brett earlier and forgotten about. Earlier that night, he'd actually thought he might meet a girl at Mike's, maybe get to fuck. "That didn't happen!" He had still been in the mood for some action, and he had known where he could purchase some. South Tacoma Way had beckoned, and Jack had answered.

Chapter 6

In any lifetime, there were ups and downs. There were times that Jack was legitimately content with being a fuck-up. He knew what he was. He didn't hide from it. Sometimes, he wore it on his sleeve like some badge of honor. He was never happy, but nobody was ever really happy. Some people were just better at deceiving themselves than others. If Jack had deception in him, he'd have told himself he was happy too.

"Maybe Paxil-poppin' soccer moms were happy. That must be a great drug. People in *Brave New World* seemed happy, with their Soma. Most of them were happy anyway. It was just a couple of them that realized their happiness was a drug-induced psychosis. That's no more of a solution than being in a coma, but who am I to talk! Nobody would accuse somebody in a coma of being happy. I don't fuckin' know. Sometimes, though, in my early twenties, I was alright."

Alright was hard to maintain. Misery was easier

to maintain. Jack knew how to keep misery around. You just kept doing whatever your current impulse or compulsion told you to do. That was it, easy! Bleakness offered comfort. Misery was both attainable and sustainable. Once you accepted misery, it immediately ceased to be such a scary proposition. Misery was normality, alright was the aberration.

Having half of a life was much scarier. "When you had somethin', you had somethin' to lose." When you had something to lose and lacked the ability to maintain it, that became a hard existence to be in. That's what alright was. Alright couldn't ever be happiness. It couldn't be happiness because the moment you realized you were alright, you also realized that you couldn't be alright for long. Pain would be along soon, and there was nothing you could do to stop it.

Nobody Jack ever knew could maintain alright, but Jack liked remembering the alright times just the same. He was nostalgic. He really didn't know why. "Yes I fuckin' do! You fuckin' idiot. Why are you the one tellin' my story anyways! I mean, I'm right fuckin' here. Why ain't I the one tellin' it? Anyway, nostalgia for the alright times happens because nobody can take the alright times that happened in the past away from you. You don't have to worry about when pain is going to start because it already happened. You already know when the pain started.

You never have to relive the pain and misery when you're rememberin' the alright times. You just live in the alright times, and never go to the pain and misery times. That's why. Duh!"

Jack couldn't remember exactly what had happened with Beth while he was in prison. She had been around, then she hadn't. He knew being with her had been the most alright time of his life. He figured he bore some of the blame for what he assumed was a breakup, maybe even most of it, but he just really didn't understand what had happened there.

The day after the party at Mike's place, Jack had picked up the handset to the phone in his mom's kitchen and dialed a number from memory. The last time he had dialed that number, she hadn't picked up, so he had just stopped calling. That day, she had picked up.

"Hello." She'd sounded a little annoyed.

"Ha, what's up," he'd said.

"Jack! Oh my fucking God! Where are you!"

"I'm out. I'm at my mom's. I wasn't sure if I should call."

"Don't go anywhere. I'll be there in twenty minutes."

Chapter 7

She had worn old Levi's, a plain white t-shirt, and her black hair tied up in a handkerchief. She hadn't bothered to look in her bathroom vanity before she had run out the door. She had slid on the loosely tied Pumas she ran errands in and grabbed her wallet and keys. On the way out of her apartment, she had ignored a hello from an annoying neighbor, and on the drive, she had ignored most of the traffic laws designed to keep people safe. It wasn't that Jack had called and she had come running. She hadn't known if she was running to a fight or a reunion. He'd blown her off, and for a long time she'd avoided confronting him about it, but then she had buzzed with anticipation, and her brain had raced with possible scenarios.

That day, Beth and Jack had never really figured out who was to blame for their breakup. They had never really been able to determine if there even *had* been a breakup. As such, they had just tried to pick up where they'd left off.

Jack's cigarettes had almost been gone again, and he hadn't had much luck locating a job. Jobs had never really been something Jack did well. He hadn't been drinking, and he hadn't been using any recreational drugs, but he was pretty sure that he should have been back on his Lithium. Getting money to go to the community clinic hadn't really seemed to be a priority right at that moment, though. Beth would have bought his prescription for him if he'd asked, but he' had already been living for months in an apartment that she had paid for and eating food that she had bought. He had figured the least he could do was take care of his own nicotine and medication needs. That was what he had told himself, but the cost of his Lithium prescription had been much cheaper than food or rent, so he had to concede that his reason had just been a deceptive self-justification.

In reality, being non-compliant with his medication had been a passive-aggressive way to sabotage himself. He'd been diagnosed with bipolar disorder, but he had never believed that diagnosis, and not filling his Lithium was his way of rejecting it. Somehow, he had found money for cigarettes every day, but failed to come up with five bucks for a month's supply of Lithium.

Whether he was compliant with his medication hadn't mattered much longer anyway. Whether he believed his bipolar diagnosis had similarly ceased to matter much. Within six months of being released from McNeil, he had walked away from Beth and toward desolation. She'd said something that had hurt his pride. No, it was more than that; she'd genuinely emasculated him, and when she had, his brain had started buzzing. No matter what he had tried, it wouldn't be quiet. Wounded or not, he had been too sensitive, and she had done everything within reason to amend the situation, but it hadn't mattered to Jack.

His mind had clung so obsessively to her words that seeing her brought a strange fusion of hurt pride, resentment, and anger. Eventually, just the thought that they both occupied planet earth had become aggravating to him. He hadn't chosen not to forgive her; he had been genuinely incapable of forgiving her. Within days, he'd become so resentful toward her that he simply hadn't been able to stick around. The thought to disappear had begun as a juvenile fantasy to get back at Beth. He had been incapable of feeling better, but he was confident he could make her feel worse. Over several weeks of planning, it had grown into a full-blown plan to cut and run. The plan itself had developed a life of its own and became a quest for self-reliance. Once his obsessive, impulsive brain had started buzzing about it, there had been no stopping him. Beth had no longer mattered to him. She had just become the lady who said the thing no woman was allowed to say to a man. With that, he had been off again.

Chapter 8

He had left when she was at work, on foot, with just a backpack of clothes and essentials like his toothbrush and deodorant. He'd had his wallet, his expired driver's license, and about two hundred bucks he'd squirreled away. Enough of his things were gone that Beth had known he'd left on purpose, but so much had been left behind that she had assumed he'd be back within a few days. Beth had been concerned, even worried, but most of all sad and betrayed. It had only been a few weeks since Mike's funeral, and she had guessed Jack was off on a planned bender. Beyond her own hurt feelings, her main concern had been that Jack would once again wind up in prison, or dead.

For a few days, she had kept her hopes up. She had still been angry—of course she had been—but she had been in love with him. She had understood that he was selfish and juvenile, and that to be with him, she'd always have to accept the hurt he did her and apologize for any she inflicted on him, no matter how slight. By day four, her growing worry for Jack's wellbeing had largely replaced her hurt feelings, and she had sufficiently subjugated that rational part of her mind that screamed at her to let him go.

That time, Beth had spent months haunting the local shelters and missions looking for him. His two remaining best friends had still been in prison, so she had sought out people that were no more than casual acquaintances of his to no avail. Of course, she had called his mom, who had been just as baffled and distraught. She had called local jails, local hospitals, and, finally, local morgues. That time, it hadn't been so easy for her, or anyone else, to find him.

Chapter 9

Jack had sought out the company of others like himself. It hadn't taken long. It hadn't taken long for him to start drinking again either. Beth had been on graves, which had worked out pretty well for Jack. They had both slept in every day. Beth because she was tired from work, and Jack because he was too hung over to drag himself out of bed. Jack had thought she didn't know that he was drinking every night she went to work. He had normally passed out an hour or so before she came home from her shift. Despite being blacked out, he'd been pretty successful in disposing of his empty bottles before she came home. Jack hadn't realized that a person who drinks all night sweats it out in their sleep. He hadn't realized that a person who drinks all night exhales it into the air as they sleep. So, he hadn't realized she knew, but she had.

Mostly, they had only seen each other before she went to work, or on her days off. Before she went to work, they'd played cards, or board games.

Sometimes, they'd watched prime time TV. All the time he had sat, almost annoyed, waiting for Beth to grab her keys and purse, and head out the door to work. Then he had been off to the convenience store for a few forties of his favorite malt liquor, which at that point was whatever was $1.99 a bottle and strong.

Some of the homeless crusty punks who hung out at Wright Park came over on nights like that. Sometimes he'd gotten too drunk and there had been fights. Sometimes he'd gotten too drunk, and they'd ripped off a bunch of Beth's shit. At no time had he gotten too drunk to fuck Kristy, the crusty punk girl that had routinely came over with the crusty punk guys. No one had called her Kristy; they had all just called her Krusty, sometimes Krusty the Clown. She hadn't been ugly or fat, but she hadn't been beautiful or thin, either. Jack had come out of more than one blackout to find his pants down and her on his lap, grinding him. Usually, her tongue had already been shoved into his mouth. Always, her black jeans and bullet belt had dangled around one of her ankles. All Jack had been able to taste was the PBR she had been drinking and the GPCs she'd been smoking. All Jack had been able to feel was a huge thick bush on his hard cock. Jack had never fucked Krusty, but after Beth had called him an unemployed loser, he had seriously considered it.

Krusty the Clown and her huge thick bush had never persuaded Jack to fuck, but her lifestyle had convinced him that he needed a change of scenery.

Chapter 10

I t was funny how well a homeless person could live. There were a variety of homeless people. There were, of course, the gimmies, who were constantly out for handouts. They sat on the side of the road begging for change and standing in line outside of the homeless shelters for hours just to sleep on a shitty cot in a room with a hundred other smelly guys. On nights Jack spent in shelters, he had been able to hear twenty other guys jerking off at any given time. Anyone who thought prison was scary had never spent the night in a homeless shelter. There were the crazy people, who just roamed the streets without any purpose whatsoever. Then, there were the working homeless. If they were named appropriately, they'd be the thieving homeless, but Jack just called them The Johnson Family. Their signs would say, "will work for food," but their motive was always to get into your house, your car, or anywhere they could rip something off. If they couldn't get into your house or your car, a tool shed was also a treasure trove. Even a good plant, repotted and transported correctly, had a street value if you knew where to sell it.

The working homeless had drinking and drug problems to support, and while they were habitually dirty, they rarely slept in the mud. As a matter of fact, most of these people could make rent at a motel with weekly rates if they didn't smoke, slam, and drink the proceeds of all their hard work. Staying drunk and high most hours of the day required sacrifices to be made. The main sacrifices were a normal standard of life, and bathing. Jack had fit right in.

"After the lifestyle chose me, I sometimes found myself wonderin' why people pay for things that can regularly be acquired for free. Things that could not be obtained for free were fairly easy to steal, and a covered place to crash was never more than a broken window or half-full newspaper bin away." Jack's Johnson Family lifestyle had been part pioneering, part piracy, and all lunacy.

The story of the west was the story of pioneering. The people who settled the west were the offspring of the original European colonists of North America. Nobody claimed those pioneering Europeans were the first people to inhabit the continent, nor that they had rightful claim to much of the land they had taken; only that wanderlust and lunacy, along with whiskey and laudanum, had fueled their hairbrained, ill-conceived westward expansion. Later immigrants to the United States had clung to the eastern cities like life preservers, but psychotic, intoxicated American pioneers had set off into the wilderness with only what they could carry on their wagons. Walking into the Rocky Mountains with your spouse, children, and everything you owned on a rolling wooden shoe box took a certain sort of person.

When humans move out into the solar system, and settle Mars, descendants of pioneers will be at the helms of the first ships to hit Martian soil. Jack was such a descendant, and if he'd been born in 2170 instead of 1970, he might have been at one of those helms. It's more likely that he'd be pushing a mop or washing the dishes in the galley, but he'd have been on that ship somewhere.

His pioneer ancestors had pushed into country they'd never seen that was foreign to them. Since then, the world had shrunk. There was no more west to explore, just a huge ocean. Nevertheless, Jack had survived on nothing but intoxicants and balls. Instead of living off the land, the way his ancestors had, he had lived off the underside of society in country that was new and foreign indeed. Cities were his wilderness, and resources in his wilderness had been plentiful, and ripe for the picking. All that had been required of him were the guts to go out there and grab what he wanted. And at the end of the day, instead of building a fire next to his horses and wagon, he'd built it in an empty freight car or an apartment complex still under construction. Hardship had become a sort of salvation. He had felt kinship with his own ancestry, as well as the punks that he had shared his food, drugs, and sometimes even his sleeping bag with.

Right around October, it had started to get a little too chilly to be comfortable living outside in Seattle, and so, they had done like the birds do. They had migrated south for the winter.

Chapter 11

This migration south hadn't been a product of Jack's genius, regardless of how much he'd like to take credit for it. It was a time-honored tradition of the homeless punks. Seattle was the place to be in the summer. Its climate was mild, and there was plenty of free food. There were lots of upper middle-class people to rob. Also, those same people wore their liberal socioeconomic guilt on their sleeves like badges of honor, so most of the time they just gave you money. Winter in Seattle, however, was just a little too cold and wet for outdoor living. Even for somebody from the northwest, like Jack was, living outside in the winter was a non-starter.

Jack's new girlfriend had been suited perfectly for outside living. Marie had had an Antischism tattoo on her chest, waist-length black dreadlocks, and a Doom back patch on her sleeveless black denim jacket. She'd had gorgeous brown eyes. Despite her Latino ancestry, an entire summer outdoors, and the inevitable thin layer of dirt and sweat covering her, she'd still had extremely pale skin.

She had been low-maintenance in every way without being a tomboy. As a matter of fact, for a homeless, crusty punk girl, she had been quite feminine. She'd had a pretty face, which Jack later realized was inexplicably a cross between Salma Hayek and a valley girl. Jack hadn't known it, largely because Jack and Marie had never talked about themselves or backgrounds, but Marie's mom had been a white, blond lady who was a cheerleader in high school. But again, Jack had never known one thing about Marie's family, past, or whatever else there was to know about her. She'd been from Eastern Washington—Pasco in the Tri-Cities, to be exact. He knew that much. She hadn't known where he was from. She had assumed Seattle, since that was where they had met. The past was the past, and you couldn't change it, so why bother talking about it? That had been their rule, and it had worked for them.

Pretty as it was, almost nobody ever saw Marie's face because her dreadlocks had constantly hung in front of it. She'd had nice tits too—big, but not too big—and a round ass. Almost nobody ever saw those either, because, again, her dreadlocks had hung down over all that, too. The oversized jeans and Anti Cimex t-shirt she'd always worn also didn't properly frame an otherwise great body.

Living outside had worked for Marie. She had never looked emaciated. Quite the opposite; she had looked like someone who worked outside all day. That is, she'd been tan, dirty, weather beaten, and muscular. She had been thick in the right spots and thin in the right spots, too. And she hadn't just looked tough; she was legitimately potent. During their time together, Jack had been forced to pull her off three different girls that had made the mistake of mouthing off to her. One time, in the parking lot of a shopping mall, Jack had watched Marie dismantle two preppy girls with Nordstrom bags at the same time.

Marie had fucked on her period, smoked while you went down on her, and stolen her tampons from Walgreens. Having a bottle and a pack of cigarettes had made her happy. If she was able to get to a punk show, so much the better, and if she was able to squeeze a cock into the equation, it was a magical night in Marie's world. In a lot of ways, she had been the perfect woman, all the stuff guys loved about girls and none of the bullshit.

When a homeless man was alone in a nasty sleeping bag, the stench could be pungent, but when a homeless man and woman fucked in a nasty sleeping bag, the smell could be unbearable. Amazingly, you did get used to that, too, and that was the life. Right then, Jack hadn't even been able to tell how bad their sleeping bag stunk. They hadn't washed it in weeks, and neither of them had showered in days. He'd hated thinking about the gross things living in it, but none of that had stopped him from fucking Marie in it. Besides, the friction of a cock repeatedly slamming into a pussy had produced a smell that was more pleasant than any smell the two of them could have produced alone.

Hopping train cars had been the preferred way to migrate from place to place, and Jack and Marie had found themselves in a mostly empty freight car travelling through the part of the thick Oregon wilderness where you started to see the occasional palm tree. "A fuckin' palm tree in Oregon! But seriously, there it was. Then there were a handful more, and then we were definitely in California."

Jack had thought that maybe, when they got off that train, they'd splurge for a motel room and do a load of laundry at the local cleaners. He had started trying to work out where they were on his gas station map. It was a roadmap with very few landmarks, and they had been on a train, not an interstate. Working out where they were had seemed next to impossible, so Jack had just asked Marie if she wanted to hop off at the next town they passed. Jack had thought that, every couple of weeks, it was nice to knock some of the loose dirt off with a shower. He wasn't entirely sure what

Marie had thought about his suggestion, but she liked drinking and fucking in the shower. Plus, a warm room from time to time wasn't bad, either.

It was a different life than the one he'd been living, and he'd felt self-sufficient for the first time since being in prison. At the same time, Jack recognized it hadn't just been about a change of scenery or self-sufficiency. He'd been running from himself, plain and simple. He'd been hiding, too. He'd been hiding from everyone he had ever known. That is, everyone except Todd.

One day, Jack had picked up a phone, punched in the stolen calling card number he'd been using, and dialed Todd's old number. To Jack's surprise, Todd had picked up. He must have had someone pay his phone bill while he was locked up. Jack hadn't bothered to ask. There had been so much else to catch up on that how Todd had kept his old phone number hadn't seemed important.

Since being released, he'd been doing what he had always done: keeping tabs on people, relaying messages, and most importantly, keeping up connections with the crew. He had told Jack that Beth thought he was dead, and that she'd been searching for him for months. Todd was the only one Jack had had the balls to call, but he'd been running from him, too. Todd was a link to Jack's previous codependent life. He was a link to Jack's parents, his friends, and Beth. Jack knew that if he had let those people bail him out, he'd have been right back behind institution walls, telling some headshrinker about his plans for creating a normal life when he got out.

Jack had still been angry at Beth, but all the shenanigans he had pulled at her apartment before he had bailed hadn't made him feel better. Nor had his new life living outside. His new life had given him a sense of self-sufficiency that he'd never felt, not even at McNeil, but it hadn't fixed the wound Beth had inflicted on him. He knew that, if confronted, she'd have claimed he'd done worse to her, and she would have probably been right. Jack was used to feeling anger, but when she'd emasculated him, she'd created a whole new emotion in him. It had been anger fused with wounded pride. Jack had continued to lack the ability to forgive Beth, and mention of her name had still produced a dull ache of emotional pain that had manifested physically in his chest. Jack had given Todd explicit instructions to tell his mom that he was alive and well, but that he was forbidden from telling Beth that he was alive.

Jack had been in love with Beth, but as far as he could tell, people could fool themselves into loving just about anyone. Was love a magical force, something that conquered all? Was it just the name we assigned to a group of biochemical processes that happened in every human? Either way, Jack had continued to hurt; he had thought it only fair that she continued to hurt as well. Other than that, he'd had no feelings about her one way or the other at that time.

After that, Jack hadn't even been able to bring himself to call Todd again. It had been easier for him avoid his old life altogether.

Inches away from him, the aroma of fortified wine had been unmistakable.

"Do you want a pull off this?" Marie had said as her arm extended toward him.

One thing that tasted worse than Orange-Jubilee-flavored Mad Dog was warm Orange-Jubilee-flavored Mad Dog, and the only thing that tasted worse than warm Orange-Jubilee-flavored Mad Dog was warm Orange-Jubilee-flavored Mad Dog full of your homeless girlfriend's backwash, but you even got used to that.

They'd hopped a train outside of Oakland after a few weeks in San Francisco. San Fran was a nice place to stop for a few weeks. It stayed warm a little longer than Seattle, and it got warm earlier in the spring, so the routine was to come into town again on the way back to Seattle for a few weeks. The ultimate destination for the migrating gutter punks was, of course, Los Angeles. It was a good place to lay low. People there were so self-absorbed that anybody else's existence barely registered on their radar.

It wasn't just self-absorbed entertainment industry types that helped make you largely invisible. LA was legitimately dangerous. Even in the early nineties, after the peak of the crack epidemic, Compton and Watts, similar to Tacoma, had remained hives of the crack trade and gang wars of the eighties. LA was also very segregated, and full of invisible borders. You could practically spit into El Sereno from the sundown town of South Pasadena, but no white people ever went south of Alhambra Road, and no Mexicans went north of it. The only exceptions were middle-class whites purchasing drugs from Mexican gang members during daylight hours and Mexican women cleaning rich white people's houses. White people bought heroin, meth, coke, and anything else that came out of LA ghettos, and then scurried back to their white sanctuaries. In simultaneous contrast, Mexican women caught their buses, cleaning supplies in hand, back home before Mr. Important Esq. returned from a long day of being a senior partner at his prestigious law firm.

Dirty, middle-aged alcoholics who all bore a striking resemblance to Charles Bukowski roamed back and forth from the dive bars down by skid row to the old man hotels with weekly rates in

Hollywood. Any place with a liquor store on the block and low weekly rates was fair game. The inebriated old man herd had migrated in twos and threes and engaged in casual violence at nearly every intersection. All this just scratched the surface of the underside of LA, and that was just the street crime that happened in full view of the world. What happened in the residences of LA was, without a doubt, just as, if not more, sordid as what happened out in the open. The LAPD had bigger problems than small bands of homeless punks stealing beer and peanut butter from the Vons. Indeed, they had barely even taken notice of them.

Jack and Marie had settled into Hollywood. The irony of Hollywood was that it happened to be the most anonymous location on earth. Nobody noticed you there, ever, not even if you levitated six feet off the ground with your hair on fire and flew back and forth between Vine and Sycamore on Hollywood Boulevard. It was the perfect place to be lost. It was also the perfect place to repetitively commit low-level crime. A tourist's stolen purse was forgotten before the bag snatcher was off the block. You often found the offender literally on the next block pilfering the thing for anything of value and discarding whatever remained. Jack had used to wonder how many tourists found their own stolen bags empty and abandoned a hundred feet from where they had been snatched.

Out in the beach towns like Santa Monica, homeless punks drew too much attention. Those beach cops always hassled them, except in Venice. People at Venice Beach couldn't have cared less if homeless punks slept on the beach in the middle of the day, but robbing tourists was not quite as simple, or tolerated. Still, when Jack had gone out there, he had almost been able to see an opportunity. He'd been convinced that he could sell clam shells on Venice Beach. His plan had been to collect clam shells on the beach, buy a cheap set of craft paints at the dollar store, and paint little pictures on the smooth inside part of the shells. Finding a card table with collapsible legs would be fairly easy, and then he would just sell each one for five bucks. Jack had some talent for drawing and, based on the other garbage that people bought on Venice Beach, he had figured he could clear fifty or sixty bucks a day. That was more than enough to rent a room in a house, as well as cover the cost of beer and smokes. Sadly, Jack's epiphany had never been realized, as Marie had hated the beach, and urged their return to Hollywood every time they were there for more than an hour.

Marie hadn't loved it, but going to the beach once or twice a week was nice. During those weeks, before they moved on to the valley, when a night at an old man hotel was out of the question for lack of funds, the beach had been the only place to get a shower. Plus, you could head out there in the morning, go to a Target on the way, steal some swimming trunks, drop off your nasty clothes at the laundromat, put on your beach gear, and hang out at the beach all day.

Again, Marie had sort of hated the beach, and she really hadn't liked getting ocean water in her dreadlocks, but she had looked great in the bikinis they stole for her. Since they'd had no use for swimming trunks and bikinis the rest of the time, and nowhere to store them, they had just thrown them out at the laundromat when they went back for their clothes. Sometimes, Marie had kept wearing the bikini bottoms as underwear, but the tops had served no purpose except on the beach. Marie's tits had been too big to be properly supported by a bikini top.

Because they had constantly disposed of swimwear, Marie had gotten a new bikini every time they went to the beach. One time, they had gotten her a low-waisted two-piece with yellow polka dots that tied in the front—very retro. She had looked like Raquel Welch in the sixties. That is, if Raquel Welch had been covered in tattoos and had waist-length black dreadlocks and a bottle of Night Train. Another time, it had been a more of a classic fit one. The bottoms had had side-ties and little pictures of ice cream cones on a turquoise background. The color and print had been ridiculous. It was something a fourteen-year-old would have worn. They had actually gotten it in the girl's section. Marie, a fully-developed woman, had managed to get into the largest girl's size they carried. There had been a plainclothes security guard near the women's section, so Marie had been forced to make do in the girl's section. Her ass had barely fit into the bottoms, even when she tied it loose, and her tits hadn't fit into the top in any meaningful way. Jack had seen her nipples peeking out of the top all day long.

She may not have excelled at actually going in the water, but she had been great at drawing attention while she lay on stolen beach towels with a bottle of whatever fortified wine they had stolen from the liquor store. Something about the tattoos and black dreadlocks as the backdrop for those brightly colored bikinis had really gotten guys' attention. The day with the ice cream cone bikini had been the worst. In that little girl's bikini, with a cigarette hanging of her mouth and a bottle in her hand, Marie had looked like the baddest high school girl in the world, and it had really brought out the pedophile lin the male beachgoers.

All in all, those beach days had been the best

times Jack could remember. Sometimes, he had even forgotten who they were altogether. He had imagined those short interludes were something like what normal people experienced most of the time. Those days had always had to end though. Sometime near dusk, they'd needed to make their way back to the laundromat, and then get a bus back to Hollywood.

The people at the laundromat had hated them— not just the employees, but the customers, too. They had stayed long enough to run fast wash cycles in the morning before putting all their stuff in one dryer, setting it, and leaving. One of two things always happened during their absence. Either customers had complained, and one of the employees had removed their stuff from the dryer, or somebody had just taken their stuff out and thrown it on a table or on top of a front-loading machine. Either way, Jack couldn't have cared less. Nobody was going to steal their clothes, and the laundromat employees had probably been too scared of them to throw them out.

The main problem with LA at that time for Jack and Marie had been that there was very little in the way of squats. Anything inside of the city had almost always been occupied, and when you found somewhere decent, somebody always ruined it by vandalizing a neighbor's car or throwing a bottle through somebody's living room window. That had always brought LAPD prematurely, and the squat would be blown for everyone. Even if they kept to themselves, the cops had come along within a week or two, booting them back onto the street. "Fuck, man, the homeless punks in Pittsburgh and Detroit must have it made. Half the houses in them cities are abandoned. I could raise kids in a squattin' environment like that."

The condemned house at the corner of Fountain and Lodi, the one with the fire hydrant out front, had been blown for them. It had been perfect. It had been walking distance to a grocery store and several liquor stores. Getting up to Hollywood Boulevard for your daily tourist hunting had been similarly easy.

Best of all, it had only been about a fifteen-minute walk from the old Raji's. The one in the Hastings Hotel. They'd had punk bands all the time, and any night that they could afford it, they had drank at Raji's. Their best days in LA had been at Venice Beach, but their best nights in LA had been at Raji's, specifically when GG Allin had played there. They'd smoked some meth with a random guy in the alley behind the club. He'd had a mohawk and a Discharge t-shirt. They had never gotten his name.

Jack had noticed Marie grinding up on the mo-hawk guy during the show, so while GG Allin had played "Die When You Die", he had taken Marie to the men's toilet, and waived the mohawk guy over. The toilet stall was covered in band stickers and graffiti, and it had smelled exactly how every other men's toilet in a punk rock club smelled. She had gone down on Jack almost immediately. The mohawk guy had pulled Marie's jeans down. Jack had been able to see she was wearing the ice cream cone bikini bottoms. Jack had seen the mohawk guy start fucking her from the back, while he had watched his cock sliding in and out of her mouth. He'd loved watching her face and looking her right in the eye while she was fucking. Everyone had cummed in about sixty-seconds or less. That was the happiest he had ever seen Marie.

Later that night, one of the punk kids at the squat had thought it would be cool to throw a Molotov cocktail he'd made out of an old pair of boxers and a half-empty vodka bottle at the neighbor's house. The bushes and the side of the house had lit up pretty fast, but the fire had died down on its own almost immediately. LAFD hadn't even needed to use the fire hydrant out in front of the squat. Nevertheless, the Hollywood squat at Fountain and Lodi was over. After that Jack and Marie had moved to the valley.

Jack and Marie had never talked about the past, and they had certainly never talked about the future. He hadn't wondered where Marie came from, and he had been wholly unconcerned with where she'd be after they parted company. Marie was like somebody that you hit it off with during a three-day meth binge and then went on a two-month crime spree with. Their personalities had fit, hand in glove. He'd had more fun with her than any other human before or after. She had been the insane person you spent every second of an entire summer with and then never saw again. She'd been the guy you sucked off just to see what it would be like. She had existed in Jack's then present, but was ultimately a memory to be hidden away in a secret place of his mind for all time and eternity. Jack loved what she was, what they had shared, and he'd tried not to pollute that by wondering about her past or future. She had done the same.

While Jack had never wondered if Marie would be alright in the future, he had often wondered what the future held for some of the other people in the squat. Even if Jack had concerned himself with Marie's future, there would have been no need. Marie was made of tougher stuff. Her insides were as tough as her tanned weather-beaten skin. In sixty years, Marie would still be Marie, doing Marie things, just like she had been that day. During the time Jack spent in LA that first summer, he had realized that most of the other punks in that squat were actually still just kids. That is, most of them were still minors, just runaways.

Jack had had no business worrying about them. After all, he had been perhaps the least functional human being among them. Nonetheless, he had played out sad possible scenarios in his head for each of them. One time, in that abandoned stucco piece of shit that they found in Van Nuys, Jack had taken a head count of fourteen, including Marie and himself. He had noticed that only three other people in that squat were over the age of eighteen. Some had come from legitimately poor circumstances, and if one of them had ever managed to find a job washing dishes somewhere and paying rent in some studio apartment somewhere they'd have been one of the lucky few. That would have been a success story of sorts, but that certainly wasn't what the future had in store for all of these kids. The remainder would eventually be locked up somewhere or dead prematurely. Jack was fucked up, but he knew how to get by. Those kids, he had surmised, were doomed.

At twenty-three, Jack had been the second oldest one there. Jack was a Sagittarius and it was December, which had meant that in a few days he'd be twenty-four. Marie was twenty-three and a Pisces. Obviously, they had gotten along great. Beth had been an Aries, and Jack had loved her even when he hadn't gotten along with her. But Marie hadn't really been someone you fell in love with; she had been a companion and a buddy. Your buddy that you fucked and who kept you company until one of you got locked up for a month of two. If and when that happened, she'd be gone. She'd find the next guy. There had been no illusions about what sort of relationship they had. It was the type of relationship that street people had with each other. Out there, you just needed something to cling on to, and so you grabbed the best-looking thing in the squat. And when they disappeared, nobody waited too long before grabbing something else to keep them company. It was understood.

Jack had had aspirations for the near future, but only the near future. He always did. Marie had had no aspirations for the future, near or far, and she never had. She probably never would. She'd been one of those broken-home types. Abuse, addiction, and molestation had not been taboo subjects in her home, not that her and Jack ever talked about it. Hardship was what she had expected from life, and it had never occurred to her that things could be better for her. She had floated into alcoholism, desolation, and homelessness almost like it was the natural progression of all human life, just the same way that someone else might finish high school, get a job, and go to college. In contrast, Jack's upbringing had been functional, if a little coddled. Marie had stayed right about where she started and had no plans beyond that point. Jack had lost ground from where he'd started, but he was always formulating a plan for the near future to claw his way from pathetic back to mediocre.

Chapter 12

T he Van Nuys squat had actually been sort of cozy. The pack they were travelling with had actually stayed there several times. The first time it had been good for a couple of weeks. Then the cops had come along and booted them, but what Jack had realized about that place was that it was in the wastelands of Los Angeles. Nobody really cared what happened out there. If a cop showed up to investigate a neighbor's complaint about squatters, it was just so they could check a box on a report. Even the neighbors that complained probably did so as a mechanical and conditioned response, just a simple exercise of societal norms. Their hearts just weren't in it. Jack had been able to tell that much.

The neighborhood was the remnants of some sprawling postwar subdivision of tract houses, little boxes on the hillside made of ticky-tacky.Needless to say, they all looked just the same. Most had moved on, leaving the neighborhood for the earth to reclaim. A few had stuck around, probably because their houses had effectively become unsellable. It must have been one of the swankier suburban subdivisions, because postwar tract houses were notoriously cheap and small. Every house in their subdivision was one of those midcentury modern, split-level ranch houses. The outsides hadn't looked like much, but they had been shockingly large on the inside with high ceilings and all.

The one they had settled into must have been the jewel of the neighborhood once upon a time. It was a four-bedroom, two-bathroom place. Nobody had been able to tell what color it had been. Any surviving paint that had managed to stay attached to the exterior of the house had peeled badly, and the sun had long since baked any identifiable color off. Sometimes, when Jack had looked at it, he thought it had been blue with white trim, but other times, he thought it had been yellow all over. Whatever color it had been, by that time it had simply become the color of some redneck's stained wife-beater.

It was also the only one Jack had seen in the neighborhood with an inground pool. It was small, but it was an inground pool nonetheless. All the yards there were small, and their house was no exception. Jack assumed some hard-working middle-class suburbanite had saved and saved until he could afford to put that pool in. It had probably been the crowning achievement of his life. How sad that it had ended up just a concrete hole lined with dirt, bottom covered with broken bricks and random castoff garbage.

It had taken several complaints from the few neighbors that did still live there before the cops had even bothered dispatching a cruiser to send them packing. Jack had actually realized it by mistake. In Hollywood, they had lived on the streets a lot of the time, literally on the streets. They'd had the Fountain and Lodi squat for a while, but a lot of the time you found them sleeping anywhere from under an overpass to inside of newspaper bins. Sometimes, they had just slept under the sheltered parts of doorways in alleys.There was one time Jack and Marie had broken into someone's tool shed and slept there. Often times, they'd gotten too drunk and just passed out in a parking lot somewhere. If a car stayed in one secluded spot for more than a day or two, to them it had been an open invitation to not only vandalize and rob it but to fuck and get some sleep in it.

They had towed their sleeping bags around with them because they hadn't known where they were going to be crashing on any given night. Also, on the rare occasions they had left their few belongings hidden somewhere, it had been pretty normal for those belongings to be gone when they came back. Why their things had disappeared, Jack never really understood. To any normal person, their ragged backpacks and ratty sleeping bags would have been garbage. The garbage was likely where they had ended up when they disappeared. Jack suspected that those disappearances had been mean-spirited and not just people innocently disposing of what they had assumed was garbage. When their things disappeared, they had never turned up in a nearby dumpster. Any normal person would have disposed of such items at their earliest convenience if they were just innocently disposing of roadside crap.

Jack understood a lot of things in this world. He understood why people hadn't wanted them sleeping in the abandoned house on their block. He understood why the cashier at the liquor store had stared at them from the time they walked in until they left the parking lot. But he never understood how their presence on planet earth could be so offensive to some people that they would maliciously hide their few meager possessions in an attempt to further deprive them of any comfort whatsoever. Anyway, anything you really didn't want to lose, or that you couldn't live without, had to be kept on your person at all times.

One beautifully smoggy Los Angeles afternoon that was accentuated by a belly full of fortified wine, Marie and Jack had decided to head up north to Sherman Oaks and catch a Dead and Gone show at a punk house up there. After the show, Marie and Jack had started walking back toward the city even though they had both known it would be an all-night walk at best, so Jack had asked Marie if she wanted to rip off a couple of bottles of Wild Irish Rose at the liquor store and go by the old squat instead.

They had stayed there that night, and then they had stayed for another couple weeks after that. The cops hadn't even bothered to remove any of the stuff they'd left at the house from the last time they had been there. At some point, they had gone back to Hollywood to see who was still hanging around. A couple of stragglers from the old Fountain and Lodi squat came up from Hollywood to live in the Van Nuys squat. It was about two weeks before the cops had come to clear them out that time, and the time after that it had taken them eleven days. They'd spent the rest of the winter and spring popping in and out of that place. They'd stay a week or so, then clear out for a few days, only to come back again. In about mid-February, Jack had stolen one of those big coolers that people kept beer in at summer parties. It had been easy enough to find one; he had just roamed around the neighborhood until he'd seen an open garage with one inside. They'd also found an old charcoal barbeque with a sign that read "FREE" on it in front of a nearby house. Jack had put the barbeque down into the back yard's empty pool.

With the cooler, as long as they had ice, they had been able to keep perishables cold. As long as they had charcoal, they had been able to cook food, and nobody had been able to see them down there in the bottom of the pool cooking. After they had put a few lawn chairs in the pool, it also became a good place to just hang out and drink. Someone stole a little boom box from somewhere, and when they had batteries, they'd listen to the same five cassettes the four of them had between them over and over.

The barbeque and cooler meant their food stamps had finally become good for something other than trading for beer and cigarettes. Jack had made hamburgers nearly every night, and that time they had stayed there for the rest of the winter. Even better, there had never been more people than there were bedrooms after Marie and Jack reclaimed it that time. They'd kept it quiet for the most part, and the people that came through did the same. To the world, it was the frowning remnants of some idealized postwar suburbia, but to Jack and Marie, it had been a home. Nobody was getting "TR" branded on them, but if Penelope Spheeris had showed up with a camera crew it wouldn't have surprised Jack.

Whoever had owned the place apparently hadn't given a shit about it, because they had never come down and cleaned it out. Probably nobody had owned it. It had probably been abandoned. They had been close to Van Nuys, but Jack hadn't even known whether they were in a city at all or just some unincorporated part of Los Angeles County. Whatever the case, some local government most likely owned the house and just hadn't gotten around to condemning and demolishing it. "Point bein', when we got the boot from the pigs, we just left tons of shit behind, and it was always there when we came back. At the beginnin' of the summer, when it was time to head back toward Seattle, I found myself actually movin' out of the place like it was my actual house. I toiled over what I could realistically bring with me in my backpack and what had to be left to the next group of squatters to find that jewel in suburbia. Whoever they were, they were sure getting' a bargain. I left two good blankets, three t-shirts, and a pair of jeans. That, and a really fuckin' kewl Youth Brigade poster that I got free at a show. Oh yeah, we also had to leave the barbeque and cooler. Oh well, and then we were off, back to the great PNW."

Heading back north had been mostly uneventful, mostly. They were in a freight car travelling through northern California when Jack had woken up to the sound of skin slapping skin. Not three feet away from him he had seen this guy Peter, who had hopped the freight train with them, fucking Marie. Jack couldn't have cared less who Marie fucked, but the fact that they were fucking behind his back had rubbed him the wrong way.

The plan had been to get off in the Bay Area and check out a squat they'd heard about there, maybe stay a couple of weeks before they headed back to Seattle. Marie was passed out when they stopped, so Jack had gotten off the train with Peter, and they had shared a bottle of Thunderbird in some bushes near the tracks. After Jack emptied the last of the bottle, he had cracked it over Peter's unsuspecting skull, given his limp body a few swift kicks about the head and torso, and hopped back on the train. For Jack, it had begun to appear that, when he needed to club someone, a bottle was always close at hand. As soon as he had done it, he had sincerely hoped that it was the last time this behavior, that was now becoming a pattern, would occur.

The train wasn't leaving for several minutes, and Jack had watched Peter for what seemed like a long time. Peter hadn't moved. Blood had still run from his head wound onto the ground, so Jack had assumed he was still alive. "If he was fuckin' dead, the blood would stop right?" If he ever woke up, he might come looking for Jack. Peter knew they'd planned to head to Seattle over the summer. Jack knew he'd have to watch his back for the foreseeable future, but he hadn't really cared. The community in Seattle was too small to not run into people. LA was much larger than Seattle, and even there the crusty punks all knew each other. Avoiding travelling punks in Seattle was unrealistic. At a minimum, somebody coming north would bring the story with them, and Jack would have to confront any friends Peter had in Seattle—but he figured fuck them, anyway. Besides, that was all contingent on Peter waking up at all, and based on how he had looked when Jack left him, Peter being alive was a maybe proposition at best.

Death was a harsh punishment for fucking a girl that Jack had just been wasting time with, but he hadn't really cared anymore. He hadn't cared about that guy; he hadn't cared if he was dead, and he hadn't really given a shit about Marie. If he hadn't just left some guy for dead in the train yard, he would have waited a few hours to hop a different train heading east and done some exploring. He would have left Marie far behind. Instead, he had gotten back on the northbound train with Marie. It had been the only one departing at that moment, and Jack certainly couldn't hang around there any longer than he had to. About an hour out of the Bay Area, Marie had woken up from her drunken stupor.

She'd asked, "Where's Peter?"

Jack had vindictively replied, "He said your pussy was nasty and got off the train."

They hadn't done a lot of talking after that. Some time later, while the train was traveling through Oregon and the Palm trees gave way to Douglas Firs and Maples, she had told Jack that fucking Peter was a stupid drunken mistake. Jack had told her that she was his stupid drunken mistake.

What he hadn't said was that Peter was most likely lying in some bushes bleeding to death. Timing had gotten Jack back on the northbound train, but after thinking about it, it was actually a lucky turn for him. He figured that if he stayed with Marie for the time being, he could dissuade her from going back there if she was so inclined. It turned out she wasn't interested in going back to the Bay Area at that point, which was what Jack had hoped for. If he'd abandoned her and gotten on a train headed east, she might have gone back to the Bay Area. She might have found Peter. She might have figured out that Jack had done it. Right then, she had just wanted to go to Seattle and see what things would be like for the summer, and Jack had been happy to stick around with her for a little while.

Chapter 13

B y the time they'd been back in Seattle for a
few weeks Jack had been beyond bored with
the life. Their new squat had been an early century
craftsman, and no less than twenty squatters had
inhabited it at any given time. There'd been five
bedrooms, and everybody had slept wherever they
felt like. Leaving your sleeping bag in a spot in
one of the bedrooms had been no better insurance
of keeping that spot than throwing your coat on a
barstool in a crowded pub in downtown Seattle.

All the houses in central Seattle were built in
the teens and twenties, and nobody had bothered
to update them. They were cramped houses on
cramped plots of land, and even their five-bedroom
squat was likely only around fifteen hundred square
feet. Perched on the crest of Madison, at the
crossroads between Madison Valley, Capitol Hill,
the Central District, and pill hill, Jack had been
able to see most of central Seattle from the attic
crawlspace windows. That crawlspace had been

about the only spot that Jack could consistently sleep without disturbance.

Even the residents of that place had been scared of the rats in the crawlspace. Jack had been less scared of rats than he was of a shitty night's sleep. Who could have predicted that in a couple short decades, the downtown skyline would grow fivefold, and every house within his view would be worth over a million dollars, including the house he was in?

That place had never gotten busted, and he had been able to stay there for months, but it hadn't been home either. That place had been continuously occupied by squatters for years. Jack had been there before when he had lived at Beth's. Some of the people that Jack had drank with lived there. Marie had been cut from a different cloth than Jack. It seemed to him that she could, and likely would, live the rest of her life on the streets. There was no reason for her to move on when she was so content with her current situation. Squatting wasn't a phase for her, but it had been for Jack.

In the game of loserdom, Jack had been ready to level up. Some of the people he had left behind at that juncture in his life were lazy or stupid, and some of them had just been doing the best they could under fucked-up circumstances. Jack hadn't thought he was better than any of them, but he'd lost the kinship he'd felt with those people for a number of reasons. The ones that were just slumming it for the summer hadn't had his respect, and the ones that just couldn't manage any better for themselves had scared him into a future-tripping state of mind. In his mind, he could see a future where he became like them. Jack didn't like that space in his mind and had tried to keep it closed as much as possible.

Right at that time, Jack hadn't known exactly how he was going to change his circumstances, but he had known it needed to happen soon. Sleeping off his hangovers had become very dull to him anyway, so he had started waking up right when the sun came up at around six in the morning and going to an AA meeting that met in this church basement every morning at seven. Coming in every morning reeking like a brewery had sent mixed messages to the AA people. Some of them had thought he was serious about getting sober but lacked initiative, and others hadn't known what to make of his presence since he had never made a spectacle of himself like so many others that routinely came into those meetings under the influence.

He hadn't been under the influence at all, and he had preferred to just sit in the corner and mind his own business. He had just been nursing his daily hangover, and he hadn't gone there for recovery or their fellowship, either. He had gone there because he could get a couple of free doughnuts or cookies and a few cups of coffee. The sugar and caffeine had helped with the hangovers and given him enough energy to go down to the Capitol Hill Branch library, where he'd spent the mornings reading newspapers and the occasional instructional book pertaining to something he thought he might need to know how to do some day.

Shop manuals about cars had always been interesting to Jack. He also liked books about psychological warfare, manipulating people, and how to tell when people were lying, to name a few. One day, he'd found a book about lockpicking, and he had spent three days reading it cover to cover. For a small investment, a person could obtain a set of lock picks that would get them into practically any house that didn't have a dog or an alarm system. He guessed, based on his own observations, that about ninety percent of houses in central Seattle had fallen into those categories back then.

None of the information he got from those books had put any money in his pocket, though. At that time, he had still relied on his old mainstays. For food, it had been soup kitchens, free church meals, and scrounging the pastries out of the grocery store dumpsters. Nothing else had really been safe to eat out of the dumpsters, but sometimes he'd tried it anyway.

For booze and cigarettes, he had mainly employed

his time-tested technique of walking down Broadway and using a one-dollar food stamp to buy a ten-cent piece of candy or a twenty-five-cent pack of gum. If the change from a food stamp transaction was less than a dollar, the store had to give you that change back in actual coins. In other words, you got the change just like if you'd paid with real money. After about ten stops, you had enough for booze and cigarettes for the day. The little convenience store owners hadn't cared, and they had been more than happy to go along with the scam. After all, the state government reimbursed them in real dollars. Sometimes, a cool owner would let you pull the same transaction several times in a day. Even better was the rare store owner who just didn't give a fuck, and would sell Jack beer and smokes for the food stamps straight across. There had been a store like that a couple miles away in the University District, but it was a pretty long walk, so Jack had mostly just stayed close and done the store-to-store method. When he'd been too lazy to go through all that, there had always been people that would buy his stamps at half their dollar value. Marie, meanwhile, had been lazy all the time. She had always sold her food stamps at the beginning of the month, but she'd drink up all the money in a couple of days. Jack went out and did his legwork every day. Even so, the stamps usually only bought beer and smokes for a week and a half, maybe two weeks if you were frugal. That had left Jack broke for at least a couple weeks a month. Plus, Marie hadn't been able to hold onto her money for more than three days, so Jack had always ended up having to come up with another plan to support her habits as well as his.

Stealing from the local stores that let you cash in your stamps was bad public relations. Also, Jack had been trying to secretly squirrel some cash away. That meant Jack had been forced to leave the neighborhood to steal booze, which was a serious pain in the ass. It had needed to be done, though. He'd needed to keep Marie intoxicated. By that time, the thought of Marie touching him had made his skin crawl, but she hadn't seemed to notice. She hadn't really missed sex as long as she was drunk. He hadn't missed sex with her drunk or sober. She had probably been fucking somebody else in the house, anyway. She had been so plowed most of the time she could have been doing it with some other guy and thought it was Jack. She wouldn't even have known the difference.

None of it had mattered to him anymore. In the near future, he was going to be leaving all the fun of the punk rock squat behind. The sound and smell of sex happening between two intoxicated unwashed individuals had been a constant. People had not only pissed but shit in the two bathrooms, which had had no running water, an ever-present reminder of the squalor that they lived in. That was to say nothing of the lice, crabs, ants, flies, and maggots, all of which seemed to prefer to living on you instead of around the house itself.

Outside had actually been a much cleaner environment to live in because crawly things that sought out filth ran indoors to places like that squat. Jack often reflected on how filthy he had used to think Western State and Fairfax had been, but compared to the Capitol Hill squat, they had been the pinnacle of cleanliness. That whole squat was a biohazard, and everybody had caught whatever everybody else in the place had. Everybody there had been ill, but they were all just too drunk and high to notice it.

Stagnant water dripping from the ceiling onto his sleeping bag while he was trying to put it all together in his head had driven him crazy, and he'd decided then and there that living in the mental ward or behind bars was better than living in that squat. It was time for him to go back to work and get the fuck out of there. "And if I got pinched in the process, oh fuckin' well."

Chapter 14

There had been an immediate avenue open to an individual such as Jack that would bring revenue right away. And there was a reason that it was such easy money. Being a daytime burglar was a good way to end up back in the pen for a long stretch, especially for a second-time felon. There he was, barely in his mid-twenties, and if he had gotten caught once doing what he was planning on doing every day for the foreseeable future it would have cost him a few years in prison. Jack was also aware that Washington State had a "three strikes and you're out" law, and he had already had one strike. He had figured that burglary in and of itself wasn't a violent felony that would get him a second strike, but he could easily have committed a violent felony if he came into contact with someone while burglarizing a house, which would get him a second strike. Honestly, he wasn't a lawyer, so he really had no idea what might or might not get him a second strike. Considering that he may have killed that guy Peter, he had figured he was on borrowed time anyway, so he might as well go for broke.

That very next day, he had kicked in the back door of a random three-bedroom house with an attached garage. That sort of residence would be his bread and butter for a little while. That place had been in Madison Valley, a pretty average middle-class neighborhood adjacent to Capitol Hill. Everybody had been at work during the day. Nobody had owned home security systems, and there were very few dog owners. All of those factors had made the neighborhood a prime place to hit.

Dogs were the biggest deterrents, even bigger than home security systems. Security systems didn't sink their fangs into your ankle when you were already retreating. Security systems were for scaring burglars off, but there was always plenty of time to run. The alarm first sounded through the call center of the company that owned the system, and they placed a call to police dispatch. There were too many relays, and even if there was a cruiser right in the neighborhood, you still had five minutes to hide. Cops never looked too hard for people either. More than once, Jack had spent the afternoon in a local dumpster after setting off a home alarm. He probably could have popped his head up after ten minutes, but he had always stayed for extended periods of time, just to be safe.

Most criminals fucked up. They thought they could outrun the cops. Jack had known it wasn't about outrunning them. It was about staying out of sight. It was being the guy that won at hide and seek, and every neighborhood had more than enough places to hide. They couldn't look everywhere, and again, they really didn't try that hard, anyway. One time, Jack had hidden out on the roof of a convenience store. He'd jumped up onto a dumpster and climbed an exterior pipe the rest of the way up. It was right on a main street, and he had watched this cop circle the neighborhood for ten minutes, tops, looking for the prowler. "That fat fuckin' cop never even got out of his fuckin' cruiser. I could have been hidin' in the front yard of the house I was breakin' in to, and he still wouldn't have found me."

Again, though, dogs were the most problematic part of being a burglar. Cops were certainly to be avoided, but avoiding them was pretty easy. You could run from a tripped alarm. A dog, on the other hand, could injure you so you couldn't run at all. You might even have to go to the hospital, and the cops might have already alerted the ER staff to be looking for dog bites.

In fact, Jack hadn't even considered breaking into houses that had dogs at all. Most of the time, if they weren't sitting right in the yard or peeking through the front window, there were good clues that a dog might live at a given house. The lawns would be torn up or patchy. There would be chew toys in the yard. Usually, you could smell dog piss all around the house. Even if the dog that lived in a house didn't pee in the yard, other dogs would pee in front of houses where dogs lived. Jack wasn't sure why they did that. It seemed patently aggressive to mark some other dog's front yard, but they did it anyway. Either way, it had helped Jack flag houses where dogs lived. Even if you missed all the other signs, chucking a rock at the front door of a house would rouse any dog into a barking frenzy. It was also a good way to get any people that might be home to answer the front door without being seen.

The first house Jack had broken into had none of those pitfalls and a bunch of good shit to steal. Rich people's shit was too hard to move. Selling someone's expensive fine china to a pawn shop was a fool's errand. What burglar was going to sit in a house for an hour packing up dishes? Normal people's shit, on the other hand, was easy to find, easy to steal, and easy to sell. Handguns, semi-expensive jewelry, VCRs, TVs, knives, and tools were all good things to steal and sell. Normal people had an abundance of all of those sorts of items.

Those items were all relatively easy things to sell, that was true, but they were also good things to trade. Drug dealers were almost always open to trading tools and home electronics for blow, crank, junk, or whatever. The other bonus of trading those items to drug dealers was that Jack hadn't needed to risk selling them to pawn shops. There were cops whose job was to call pawn shops and look for stolen items. It was the reason pawn shops got your ID when you sell them things. Good thieves, like Jack, had found pawn shops that bought stolen items, no ID, no questions asked, but they'd gouge the thief on the price.

Sometimes, Jack had gotten desperate and sold to a straight pawn shop. There was a huge risk when it came to selling to pawn shops that did things the right way. When one of those detectives whose job it was to prowl the pawn shops looking for stolen items found one, he'd get the seller's information from the pawn shop owner, and then you were being investigated for burglary and selling stolen goods. It was always a risk, but sometimes it couldn't be avoided.

One way or the other, trading things to drug dealers meant that Jack had gotten close to market price for the items, just in illicit drugs instead of cash. He had been able to sell those drugs himself for cash on Broadway, or he had used them to get high. Better yet, he had used use them to get Marie high so that he hadn't had to talk to her. Dealing drugs on Broadway had been less risky than burglarizing homes. Seattle police didn't really care about drug commerce on Broadway, but they cared a lot about homes being burglarized.

Jack hadn't traded firearms to drug dealers, though. They always wanted firearms, but Jack had refrained from trading guns to dickhead drug dealers that he didn't like in the first place. Confrontation with drug dealers was an omnipresent threat. They were always edgy and paranoid. To Jack, it hadn't made sense to trade a gun to a local drug dealer that might very well point that gun at him a day or two later. Jack had saved the firearms for the crooked pawn shop owners.

Jack had filed the serial numbers off before he'd let anyone, especially the crooked pawn shop guys, touch them, and those crooked pawn shop guys had never known his real name. Buying defiled, stolen firearms was a big risk for them, but also for Jack. They could have lost their businesses, or even done a little time, but Jack had already had a violent felony conviction. He would have done years for selling stolen guns. Plus, picking up a second strike had scared the shit out of him. Either way, those crooked pawn shops had probably just sold those guns to the drug dealers that Jack refused to, but at least Jack hadn't done it himself.

Every time Jack had caught himself standing at a pawn shop counter when an SPD detective strolled in and started asking about stolen merchandise, he'd broken out in a cold sweat. It had happened a handful of times during his burglarizing days. Every time he'd promised himself that he'd get a job washing dishes somewhere and just accept being a poor loser like everybody else. He had just needed enough to get a place of his own and some new clothes first.

Jack had recognized the same detective at least twice. How many times had that detective seen him? From a nondescript car, that detective could have seen Jack walking in and out of the local pawn shops on an almost daily basis for months. How many times had he noticed Jack in different pawn shops around town? How much heroin had been in Jack's pocket? Had the pistols and power tools he had just sold that guy been hidden behind the counter, or were they just sitting out for the detective to see? In a mental frenzy which came on suddenly, like the first hallucination from a few hits of LSD, all those questions and more had flashed through Jack's mind on each of those occasions. All this had happened while he tried his best to keep his outward composure and appear as a casual browser looking for a good deal on a weed whacker.

Jack knew each time it happened that if the pawn shot guy had gotten pinched right then and there, he'd have rolled over on Jack in a second, and since he hadn't known Jack's name or where he lived, he'd have needed to do it while he was in the store. Every time one of those detectives hit the road, leaving Jack be, he'd promised himself: "Just until you have enough to get a place and get settled." In Jack's estimation, he was getting close to either quitting that business altogether or getting pinched. One day, a very close call had prompted Jack to get out of that game while he still had his freedom.

Chapter 15

And so, one day, Jack had just left the squat. At least, that was how it had appeared to anyone that was paying attention, including Marie. In reality, it had been about two and a half months of non-stop running, scheming, and saving when he had decided to leave. He'd managed to save a little more than two thousand dollars. He'd gotten a new state ID while he was burglarizing houses. He'd needed the ID for selling to law-abiding pawn shops.

Establishing your identity from scratch was no easy task. Jack had spent days going downtown to the county records building and filling out papers so he could get a birth certificate, then days more at the Department of Licensing getting a new ID. He had known he'd be looking for work soon, and so he had spent days more at the Social Security Administration office applying for a new Social Security Card. The Social Security card had needed to be mailed, so he had gone to the Capitol Hill post office and got a P.O. Box. He'd had more than enough money for first and last months' rent and security deposit at an apartment, but it hadn't been easy to find someone who felt like renting to an unemployed single male, especially one who had tried to pay with a stack of folded up twenty-dollar bills. Jack had needed a bank account, a checkbook, and a bank card. Jack's next stop had been the Seafirst Bank on Broadway, where he had spent another long day opening a bank account.

He had left the squat without any place to go. It hadn't mattered. He'd figured he had enough to stay at a motel until something came through. It was easier to look for an apartment living in a motel than living in a squat. For starters, there was a phone, so he had been able to get call backs from apartment managers and prospective employers. Plus, there was a shower, so he had been able to look presentable when he did show up to meet an apartment manager or prospective employer.

This was not to be one of his great disappearing acts. It was nothing in the realm of what he had pulled on Beth, his crew, or his family on several occasions. When he had left them, he had done it because he hadn't been able to bear looking them in the face. At the squat, he hadn't told anybody he was leaving because he didn't give a shit about any of them, and none of them had cared about him, either. Nobody there had needed or deserved an explanation from him, not even Marie, and so he had just gone away without informing anyone.

What Marie had deserved was a little something that he could manage. In the pocket of her patch-covered sleeveless black denim jacket, he had left her two hundred dollars. Even more valuable than that was about two grams of good heroin. If she was miserable enough, she could slam all the heroin at once and just check out for good, but Marie was never miserable, so he had been sure she'd shoot the smack safely and drink up the cash in about a week or so. That had been all the goodbye he owed her, and he was pretty sure it was all the goodbye she would have wanted anyway. "God bless her, I don't believe in no God, but what the fuck ever."

The heroin had been the last of a stash he'd failed to sell before he left. Having the proceeds that selling it on the street would have brought could have been a nice chunk of change in his pocket, but the prior day's events had drastically changed his plans.

It had been a bad day that had nearly become catastrophic. He hadn't even bothered to retrieve his stash of stolen goods, which he had kept in the trunk of a broken-down Honda in an alley behind some empty house two blocks away. The heroin and two hundred bucks he had left Marie just happened to be in his pocket when he had decided to leave the squat. If they'd been with the rest of his stolen shit in the Honda, he'd have abandoned them, too.

The motel Jack had gone to was right on Aurora in the north end of the city, otherwise known as Highway 99. It was the strip where all the street hookers and pimps operated. There were also no less than a dozen rub and tug massage parlors between 80th and 125th streets. There were plenty of drugs up there, too, but mainly it was the part of the city where sex was for sale.

Jack hadn't planned on being there for more than a couple of days. The apartments he had been looking at were right back on Capitol Hill. A couple were no more than a handful of blocks away from the squat. He had wondered how conversations would go when he inevitably ran into punks from the squat. He'd even run into Marie sooner rather than later, but that would probably be more awkward for him than for her anyway. He'd had a pretty clear memory of their time together, not to mention some legitimate feelings for her. From her perspective, Jack had just been a guy she spent half of 1994 and the majority of 1995 with, mostly just a foggy blur.

At the Klose Inn, where he had decided to hole up until he found an apartment, he had been given access to fifty-seven TV channels, a phone, a shower, a bed, and lots of beer. A couple of days at the

Klose Inn had turned into a couple of weeks, and Jack had started to become one of the fixtures around the place. Somehow, finding work and an apartment had kept getting pushed out another couple of days, a week, and so on and so forth. As was his pattern, he'd worked vigilantly and socked away some money just to watch it dwindle as he became more and more sedentary and idle after achieving some level of temporary comfort. Drinking, smoking, eating, and a couple of trips to Aurora prostitutes, along with the weekly rates of the motel, had taken a serious negative toll on the balance of his newly established bank account. His savings had gone down to about thirteen hundred dollars. It was still more than enough to get a place, but he needed to find something soon if he was going to get a real apartment. If he waited much longer, his only option would be finding a room in a house with a bunch of roommates. It was true that he had been spending most of every day drinking and watching TV, but nearly every day for almost two weeks he'd also been applying for work at every greasy spoon and coffee shop on Broadway, and then following up, but nobody was offering him work. Nothing.

The day before he forked out another one hundred and fifty bucks for one more week at the Klose Inn things had just sort of fallen into place. That day, he had woken up to the phone ringing at about ten-thirty in the morning. That was early for Jack. Since leaving the squat, he had readjusted to his normal, alcoholically-inspired noon wake-up time, but he had known he needed to sound awake on the phone. The worst thing you could do when you were waiting to hear about a job or place to live was to sound like you were hung over and sleeping when you answered the phone, especially at ten thirty in the morning.

Employers had this strange notion that unemployed people woke up at six in the morning, went to Starbucks for their morning coffee, and then waited by the phone all day for someone to call and offer them a job. Jack only woke up at six in the morning for work, like burglarizing homes. Anyone that had ever been an unemployed alcoholic knew that you drank all night and slept all morning. Afternoons were the time for filling out applications. It was just common sense.

Jack had slapped himself about ten times in the face and practiced saying hello out loud for a few seconds to get that sleepy tone out of his voice before he had picked up the phone. It had been the manager of a little coffee stand called Vivace on Broadway just north of Thomas Street. The guy on the phone had asked if Jack was free for an interview that afternoon. Jack had always thought that was an odd question that prospective employers asked. He hadn't had a job. It stood to reason that his afternoon was free. Of course, Jack recognized it was just a nicety that people engage in, but the truth was, if Jack hadn't been available that afternoon, the guy on the phone would have just called the person on the next application for an interview. Jack, of course, had agreed to an interview that afternoon.

As he hung up the phone it had rang again before he could remove his hand from the receiver. Now mostly awake, he hadn't hesitated to pick it right up. The apartment manager of a building called The Gayle on Thomas Street, no more than three blocks away from the coffee shop where he had an interview, had been on the other end of the line. She'd reviewed his application and was wondering if he could come by the building that afternoon to meet with her in person. Jack had laughed at the question a little before eagerly agreeing. Being homeless was similar to being jobless, in that, when you had nowhere to live, what else could be more important than getting to an interview with somebody that might rent you an apartment?

Chapter 16

The nineties were coming to a premature close in Seattle, in what could only be described as their natural conclusion. It was the end of 1995, but the chapter on that decade had already been written. The music scene around Seattle that had been so fresh in 1990 had by then become nothing much more than a corporate grunge fusion and mutual masturbation session for the players involved. Luckily, it was about to end. Major labels, record companies, and MTV had grown tired of Seattle. Nobody cared about flannel shirts, beanies, and long hair anymore.

Without the record industry overlords pulling its strings, Seattle would soon reseed itself with a specific crop of punk bands that closed down the remainder of the decade and millennium. Seattle returned to its independent roots with the primitive and primal noises that crept in from the dark PNW forests, and for a few years, it drown-out the waning sounds of the pseudo cock rock that grunge had become. How about a Zeke record. Death Wish Kids anyone? Queue up the Murder City Devils, please!

The music industry had picked the carcass of Seattle's early nineties music scene clean to the bone. The rock stars that the grunge scene had created mostly imploded over the next several years. And at the end of it all, they didn't leave much more than a footnote on popular culture.

Before they were even done with Seattle, MTV and the record industry in general were already looking for the next big thing. By 1994, they'd found a type of punk was easily digestible by throngs of middle-class suburban white kids. Fortunately for everyone in Seattle, the dangerous war drum appeal of the new Seattle punk scene was not so easy to swallow, so this time MTV and the record executives stayed away. Once the world heard "Longview" by Green Day, the feeding frenzy was on in the Bay Area. Other than Green Day, there were certainly fewer mainstream successes among the Bay Area punk bands then there had been in Seattle, but even bands like Jawbreaker had their day in the sun.

Every year, Jack had seen less and less of the crusty punks and street kids in the U-district until eventually he had barely seen them at all. That little squat he had recently vacated seemed like the last outpost of another dying subculture.

Seattle was becoming the mecca for what would be known as tech bro culture. Back then, Jack hadn't been sure who all these people that wore collared shirts with fleece vests over them were. He had just known there were a bunch of them all of a sudden, and they all had these ID badges clipped to their belts or hanging around their necks on lanyards. All sanctimony aside, the nerds were on the march, and they were about to gentrify Jack and his ilk right out of Capitol Hill, and eventually out of Seattle altogether.

About four years later, a four-day war on the streets of Capitol Hill and Westlake Center between cops and protestors would take place. Symbolically, the nineties had, at that point, been over for years in Seattle, at least as far as the rest of the world was concerned. The WTO protests signaled the actual end of the decade, the end of the century, the end of the millennium, and the end of Seattle as a culturally relevant destination. Those last few years of the nineties were an in-between place in a city that had not come to grips with its quaint, working-class, liberal past and the role it was about to play in the new information economy.

The end of 1999 was still a ways off for Jack. While he had spent those short few days of employment at Vivace, companies like Microsoft, Amazon, and a hundred others people would soon know the names of had already been busy importing an upper-middle-class workforce from top-tier cities all over the country and bringing people from abroad on work visas.

New money, new economy, new people: they descended on Seattle like locusts on a grain field. They had signing bonuses, and were itching to spend them. Nobody local stood a chance. They were a tidal wave. They displaced everything they encountered. Unlike a tidal wave, they didn't recede and disappear. They stayed. "I didn't like what the record industry did to the Seattle music scene, but at least they had the decency to leave after they fucked it up. You can rebuild after MTV rapes your culture, but these technology fuckers ain't goin' nowhere. They're here for the duration. Seattle was over then. It's super over now."

Like so many invaders before, they claimed they brought prosperity. They claimed that their way of life was going to make things better. Just like Spanish invaders in Central America, or Roman invaders in England, they brought their culture but destroyed a way of life that the native inhabitants cherished. To native Seattleites, it seemed like all they brought were glass towers, million-dollar condo listings, and a declining quality of life for everybody not in the millionaires' club. "Right then,

I started to appreciate the plight of the Duwamish, the original native Seattleites."

To Jack, it had seemed like the money and prosperity they had brought to Seattle only ever benefitted themselves. What, he often wondered, was the point of having a top-tier city that only a top tier of citizens can enjoy? Jack wasn't necessarily smart—or educated, for that matter—but he had good instincts in great abundance. Jack's instincts on that matter couldn't have been more right. All the information economy's money and talent hadn't been able to see what Jack saw from a sidewalk coffee stand in 1995. That was that Seattle would simultaneously become the richest and poorest place imaginable. By 2022, it seemed like half the city had lived in luxury condos on the fiftieth floor, and the other half lived in tents on the sidewalk, smoking blue Fentanyl pills out of tin foil with plastic straws, outside those same luxury condo buildings. "Progress brings problems, money brings poverty, homogeneity brings its dagger right to the heart of creativity. Oh fuckin' well. Seattle.'What a pity, they've fucked up, this city where I grew up. Now, it's grown too big, and there's no room left for me.'"

From the coffee stand, for the few days he worked there, Jack had really realized how much change was actually happening in the neighborhood and

Seattle in general. He hadn't noticed it as much when he was living in squat, but at Vivace he had actually interacted directly with this new Seattle for the first time. What Jack had found even stranger was that the handful of pre-existing residents that did hang on to their place in the city were evolving to conform to the new Seattle. The gay guys that Jack had used to see hanging around at Neighbours and R Place were going to work in suits and buying apartments in the neighborhood. They'd wanted so badly to try to keep some of the neighborhood's soul intact by staying, but in so doing became what they had priorly railed against.

The neighborhood itself had become what it railed against. Bohemian, artistic, and collective became homogenized, bland, and self-centered. It was nothing new; money and the people attached to money spoiled everything. They lacked a genuine viewpoint, taste, or artistic talent. Their talent was in the acquisition of things. Somehow, they thought that if they bought fine art, they had developed taste. Or if they read a piece of philosophy, they had an opinion. In Seattle, they thought if they acquired a unique social ecosystem, they would become members of a unique social ecosystem. In reality, they just let salt water into a freshwater lake. Eventually, the city as a whole, and the entire Puget Sound to some extent, became a more watered-down version of what happened to Capitol Hill.

The coffee stand had been no place for Jack, though. Making coffee for these picky new Seattleites had been too difficult. They had always wanted skim milk in their lattes. Jack had never understood that. "Half the fuckers that wanted skim milk were already fat as shit! In which case, one whole milk latte made zero difference anyway. The other half were skinny fuckin' girls with no asses. In which case, some whole milk might have helped them grow some much-needed curves. I just don't get it. All the normal-sized people just drank their lattes with whatever we put in there." Needless to say, they hadn't liked Jack at Vivace. The customers hadn't liked him, and the employees hadn't liked him much either. Certainly, the manager that had serendipitously called Jack that fateful day at the Klose Inn hadn't liked him. Nobody there had wanted to tell him that he was fired, but after the first week he wasn't on the schedule. Jack hadn't even asked; he had just left.

His paycheck for a week of work at Vivace hadn't gone far, but it had bought him a little more time. After he had gotten some liquor and groceries for his place, his savings was down to a couple hundred bucks. The first and last month's rent had been paid, so he had at least seven weeks before he had to come up with rent. Between the Vivace paycheck and what he had in his bank account he'd had enough to pay another month's rent, and he had decided he would do that with the money. Best not to go to the manager after being there one month and tell her that he already had to use his last month's rent. Besides, there had been food at the apartment, and the power was on. He'd had a TV that he'd stolen on one of his last home prowls. He could always spare change for booze and cigarettes if he needed to, or just steal them. He hadn't been concerned about that at present. Not having a job had been concerning, but it was a concern that he wouldn't have to worry about for long.

"Dumb luck is the luxury afforded to fools, the Irish, and drunks, or some such similar shit." Luckily for Jack, he fit into all three categories. He was certainly foolish, and a drunk. Two of his grandparents were Irish, so he figured that got him into the final category. "My paraphrasin' is pretty fuckin' bad, but it's the truth and a constant fact of life for me." The downside of dumb luck was that it only kept you alive so that you were around to make even bigger mistakes than the ones that you'd needed the dumb-luck to bail you out of in the first place. It was a viscous circle that seemed to have no end, which was also a constant in Jack's life.

One day, not so long after leaving Vivace, Jack had walked down the street and seen a sign hanging in the window of a Taco Del Mar downtown that read: "HELP WANTED." In other words, slackers welcome. When a business didn't even go to the trouble to list a job opening in the newspaper, it meant a couple of things. First, the job required zero brain cells to perform. Second, as long as you weren't smoking your crack pipe while you filled out the application, they were going to hire you. That sign had been a beacon to Jack. It had been a flower in a sea of shit.

"You couldn't buy a better job than that one." It hadn't paid enough to really live on, so nobody with any aspirations in life hung around for long. "But it was also pretty gravy as far as workload." It had also been fairly simple, and the people had been pretty cool. The employees had all been burnouts, and the ones that weren't had been complete flakes. Because showing up for work seemed to be optional, the employees had always left an abundance of shifts to be filled. Compared to the other burnouts at a place like that, Jack had appeared to be an exemplary employee, and he had been able to keep a job like that as long as he wanted it. All that was required was to show up most of the time, and put in minimal effort. Jack had definitely been able to handle that.

The benefits had been pretty great too. Free food, daily tips averaging ten to fifteen bucks, otherwise known as beer and cigarette money, and, again, lenient work hours. Nobody had cared if you showed up hungover, and more often than not the manager and everybody else had been stoned out of their minds anyway. That said, there hadn't been any of the things that people normally associated with the word "benefits" in the employment context. There hadn't been any dental, medical, retirement, paid sick leave, vacation, etc.

Jack had never had any of those things before, so he hadn't given it much thought. He always saw a doctor when he was committed or locked up. One of those things, he had figured, would happen in the near future, at which time he'd see a doctor, so no problem there. He was young and had all his teeth. His nighttime grinding had flattened them out to the point that they looked like little off-white bricks instead of teeth, but he had all of them. "As far as retirement, paid sick leave, and vacation, normal people didn't get those things. Only the bourgeois fuckers got that shit."

The fall had started to feel like winter again, and with it had come that little bit of chill that made the morning bearable. Jack had preferred to work his normal night shift, but a couple times a month, he was scheduled for a morning shift. To Jack, the worst thing in the world was waking up with a nasty hangover, but he had kept drinking, and he had kept waking up, so he had kept waking up with hangovers. If the misery of a hangover had to be exacerbated by waking up in the morning, getting outside into the cool air and pissing rain, which always seemed to fall in a manner more constant and deliberate than overwhelming and sporadic, had been medicine to his hungover mind and body.

As he walked to work on one of those morning shift days, he had pondered that Taco Del Mar was a pretty perfect job for a guy like Jack, but what he hated about it was that he was starting to feel his age. He was starting to become that guy that had never really gotten it together. Lots of people spun their wheels for a few years in their young adulthood, but most of them, even most of the real trainwrecks, usually managed to move into some sort of career and normality in life. They accomplished what Jack had never been able to. They seemed to assimilate into the fabric of society. They didn't work the night shift at Taco Del Mar when they were nearly twenty-five. It didn't take one of his coworkers to tell him that he was like five years older than everybody there, but when they did, Jack's brain had been forced to confront the implications of that. In a couple of months, he'd be twenty-five, and he hadn't accomplished much, unless you counted fostering a festering addictive personality that had left him prone to any and all things addictive. That, and his career background as a monetarily disappointing small-time burglar and drug dealer. "Don't forget commitment, prison, and homelessness."

He wasn't anybody, and he was becoming less of anybody every single hour of his life. It really had bothered him. That is, what had bothered him was that he had the ability to recognize how poorly his life had gone. It had bothered him because it had also meant that he was capable of wanting things that his limited abilities could never provide.

He wasn't climbing. He wasn't even maintaining the ground he had. His wheels were spinning, but the painful downward slide of his life had commenced nonetheless. In reality, he'd been sliding down that slope for years, but in your early twenties you were sort of given a free pass to be a loser. Jack's pass had been punched, then it had been turned over and stamped on the backside despite its expiration date, and then he'd borrowed somebody else's pass. Then he had gotten that one punched too.

He hadn't had any opinion on what he should do about his situation. It had seemed even sadder that he was now depressed about being a loser amongst burnouts. Even his stoner manager had been going to night school. Jack hated the melodrama, but if somebody had told him what he was in for before he was born, he would have refused to go.

Life seemed to him to be a series of shitty and

painful situations with occasional and momentary pleasure. It was like sitting in a park on a fall morning after drinking all night, the only time Jack actually liked being awake in the morning. There was always a couple of hours between the time you ran out of beer at four, and when it went back on sale at six. When that first morning 40oz got cracked open, the smell of the brown bag always mixed with that pungent malt liquor smell. Holding the neck of the bottle as you walked to your destination always conformed the brown bag into the shape of the 40oz bottle inside. It always looked like a little missile, warhead, or torpedo wrapped like a parcel, ready for the mail. Those moments were perfect, but that wasn't life. That was respite from life.

Punishment was life. Humans adapted, and eventually they thrived on what they were fed, regardless of what it was. Jack's life was about failure, and hardship. Jack had been forced to hurt and fail to thrive, and by thrive he meant slow down his inevitable decline. He couldn't be nourished on anything else. Whenever he had been, he had shut down. Clearly, this was ironic and sad for him, but necessary and true nonetheless. "I fuckin' bet it's pretty common, too. I bet a lot of fuckers are stuck in the same shitty boat as me. Well, maybe a little better boat than mine, but still a pretty fucked-up boat"

Jack probably knew things weren't ever going to get better for him. Actually, he always figured they'd get worse, or stay equally shitty. Making it on time to his next metaphorical beating was his purpose. "Crappy food, shitty booze, nasty cigarettes, miserable job, uninhabitable livin' conditions, these are my joy!" He had enjoyed his occasional respite, but, like a Spartan warrior, he had sought only more hardship. Unlike a Spartan warrior, he had done it because life had never handed him another option. Maybe he had sought it out all along; maybe there was another option. But likely not.

Even the one with the greatest stamina for pain and failure eventually tires. Jack believed his next trip to Western State was right around the corner. It would provide some respite, but he had started to seriously desire his ultimate respite. Jack had been running for years, but hungover on that cool wet fall morning, he had known all he'd accomplished was to run in a circle right back to a locked mental ward, right back to where his story had begun.

Chapter 17

B ut that was when Jack was twenty-five. When he was thirty, he stole Dolores's Volkswagen, and drove to Utah to get some fresh air. That four-year period after Jack's trip to Utah wasn't kind to him. The saddest part of Jack's story is still to come, and the saddest part of his story you'll have.

The final time Jack was committed to Western State Hospital, he was thirty-four. The new millennium was an old story, and the world had accepted the Internet as an indispensable staple of life on planet Earth. Every time Jack had been there, or somewhere similar to there, he'd come at the discretion of the court system or doctor's authority, but on that last occasion, he'd all but come to the front door and begged to be let in.

That time, he'd lost a couple more friends, and a few more years of a remarkably wasted life. In his mind, he'd had the illusion that Beth would somehow not remember him or that she'd moved on. It had been years since he'd quietly left her apartment.

Somehow, during all those years, he'd managed to not get committed to Western State. Deinstitutiona lization had firmly taken root in the United States, and people like Jack didn't necessarily end up in the state mental hospitals with the frequency they used to. That wasn't to say he'd been living as normal people did.

Since leaving Beth's apartment that day, he'd lived as a crusty punk street migrant, a successful burglar for the first time, a successful drug dealer for the second time, and done that stretch at Fairfax before meeting Dolores. He'd lived in county jails, halfway houses, subsidized government housing, and on the streets again at least a dozen times in some seemingly unending cycle.

Since turning thirty, he'd mostly transitioned from a sporadically transient young man, who the system found resources for, into a hardened adult vagrant and criminal, who the system opted to lock up in county jails for weeks or months at a time awaiting trial on petty offenses. Typically, he wound up sentenced to weeks or months in the same county jails over and over again after being convicted of the same petty offenses over and over again.

By thirty-four, his list of misdemeanor convictions had risen to thirty or more, but Jack had long since lost count. There were no more second chances for Jack, and he'd passed the age where his antics were still cute. He'd also passed the age where his appearance still endeared him to the sort of women that had used to take pity on him.

He could never be locked up for long, because his offenses were always the petty crimes that accompanied indigency. He was never committed anymore because of deinstitutionalization, and because he'd been so mentally ill for so long his mental illness appeared to be his baseline. It was so much his baseline, and so well did he wear it by that point, that his competency to stand trial was never even raised in at least ten misdemeanor cases against him during the course of those hardest four years.

He did his time in whatever county jail he found himself, at which point he was always released onto a downtown sidewalk somewhere to resume his depressing survival hustle. The world was essentially just waiting for him to die so that, in so doing, he would solve the problem that his existence created for the people in it.

One morning, when he was thirty-four, he was roused by a corrections officer. He was in King County Jail. It took him a moment to realize that. When you woke up in different places often enough, that lackadaisical state of reassurance that most people experienced when waking up eventually disappeared. It was replaced with a skipped heartbeat and ice-cold blood shooting through one's veins, the trauma of a fight or flight response. He was put out on Fifth Avenue in downtown Seattle on a frozen February day, wearing clean but ugly clothes that had come from the jail's clothing donation room, which the jail maintained for prisoners being released without the clothes they arrived in. The clothes Jack had arrived in a few weeks earlier had been severely soiled, and were disposed of in a biohazard bin. Jack couldn't count the number of times he'd been shooed out the front door of King County Jail onto that same spot on Fifth Avenue, no direction about what to do next, no lawyer, social worker, or probation officer to point him in the direction of services he might utilize.

He'd just been released on the theft charge he'd been held on. The convenience store where he'd stolen a bag of Cheetos and 40oz of Olde English 800 had lacked functional tapes in their surveillance cameras, and they had lacked a now in-the-wind employee to come and testify to Jack committing the theft. The city had dismissed the case, but Jack didn't even know that. He had probably been informed by the jail staff or his public defender. They had probably given him court papers when he was discharged, but Jack wouldn't have bothered to read them at that point.

They were just another stack of papers to him.

Sometimes, they said he'd completed his sentence following conviction. Sometimes, they said your bail had been posted by such and such nonprofit bail fund and you were required to appear in court on such and such date. Sometimes, they said the case you were being held on had been dismissed by the city for lack of evidence. What they said didn't matter. That day, he was out. On any random day before that, he was incarcerated. Inevitably, on some day in the near future, he'd be incarcerated again. Jack had learned something about present-sense awareness and living in the now, something most supposedly successful people never figured out.

Jack had one task at that moment, and he got about it right away. He walked down to Pioneer Square, where he began rifling through the recycling bins of large downtown buildings. Truth be told, he was rifling through recycling bins during the entire walk down to Pioneer Square. He was looking for something specific. He didn't find it along the way, but after six or seven recycling bins near Pioneer Square he found what he was looking for. It was a relatively intact refrigerator box. Some office suite in the high floors above must have had to replace the refrigerator in their office's kitchenette. He carted it over to the Yesler overpass.

From past experience, Jack knew that getting a

spot under Yesler could be difficult. It was a prime spot, and people who had spots down there didn't like giving them up. That day he was lucky, and there was just enough space for his Maytag box right on the south side of the overpass. He saw some friendly familiar faces amongst the other tramps, and one or two that he actually knew fairly well. He knew as people currently camped down there disappeared, which they always did on account of being arrested or hospitalized, that he'd be able to move closer to the warmer, dryer center of the overpass within a few days. The center was where they'd get the barrel fire going at night.

Once someone staked out a spot, it was hands-off for at least a few hours at a time. The hobo code. With his new home secure, he began to prowl for anything that he could trade for a hit. It didn't take long. Jack was looking for unlocked car doors when he saw some guy at a bus stop set his backpack down next to him on the bench. Jack got a running start and was around the corner at Fourth and Washington before the guy even realized what had just happened. Within ten minutes, Jack was around the corner of the same block at City Hall Park trading the Sony Discman and a handful of CDs to the dope man for a hit of heroin. He kept the backpack.

Years back, Beth had extensively searched Pioneer

Square for Jack. She had quite unwisely walked through City Hall Park and through the Yesler overpass looking for him. He just hadn't made it there yet. She had searched almost daily for over a year, and sporadically after that. She had never really stopped looking, but after a few years, she had resigned herself to accepting that Jack might not ever resurface. One thing was for sure, she was certainly not searching the Yesler overpass all those years later.

One morning Jack woke up back in Tacoma at the Vagabond Motel."The Vagabond was actually in Lakewood, but close enough." Was it morning? Afternoon? It really didn't matter. He remembered coming there when he was fifteen to party with some people. It was the first time he had ever gotten blackout drunk. He had drunk a whole bottle of Orange Jubilee Mad Dog and some beer. That night, another guy had fucked his girlfriend. "Man, I woke up with a hangover, and a slut for a girlfriend. But whatever, I guess. I mean I went to bed with a slut for a girlfriend, I just didn't know it yet. But I definitely didn't go to bed with the hangover. I'd have noticed that!"

It didn't seem like nineteen years ago to Jack, but it had been. To Jack, memories never seemed like they had happened a long time ago. He assumed, since he spent most of the hours of the day in alcoholic blackouts, that the memories must have seemed closer in time because there was so much missing time in the interim. There was that, and the fact that nothing ever changed in Tacoma.

Things changed in Seattle. Everything changed in Seattle, but in Tacoma, nothing changed. Even the buildings were never torn down, not even the ones that should have been torn down. The run-down Taco Bell building became a check-cashing place. The Safeway that was literally falling over turned into a Goodwill. The gas station somehow transformed into a teriyaki restaurant even though the decommissioned pumps were still outside.

"Seriously, it's the fuckin' weirdest thing you ever seen. They got fuckin' outdoor tables right next to the old decommissioned pumps that still have the fuckin' Arco logo on 'em. And ain't no fuckin' place to sit inside neither cos it's a fuckin' gas station, right! They don't even have those shitty table umbrellas out there for you. Christ's sake, it's Western fuckin' Washington. Didn't those people that opened the teriyaki place think puttin' up some fuckin' umbrellas for their customers would be nice? It rains all the goddamn time here. You want to sit down and eat, and you're, like, gettin' soaked by the pissin' fuckin' rain! Good spicy chicken teriyaki though, seriously, check it out."

Certainly, the Vagabond never changed. Why

would it? As long as the rooms had four walls and working lights, teenagers would come to drink and get high with their friends. In nineteen years, it hadn't changed one iota. And it probably hadn't changed in the fifty years prior to that. Tacoma had the unique ability to remain the same no matter what happened elsewhere. That motel had remained consistently dirty, and dirty in the same fashion, for all those years.

Even the cars in Tacoma never got any newer; they'd had the same era of cars Jack's whole life, the same old shitty economy models with no options, in the same disrepair as the night that guy Lee had fucked his girlfriend all those years ago. The Vagabond had the same old lady owner sitting at the front counter renting rooms, just sitting there smoking cigarettes for nineteen years, and she hadn't aged a day. Of course, she hadn't gotten any younger, either. "That bitch was old and ugly when I was fifteen, and she was old and ugly when I was thirty-four. She'll probably be old and ugly fifty years from now when I'm in a fuckin' box of abandoned ash sitting' on a shelf at the county crematorium. God, that bitch is ugly as puke, old as shit too!"

Just when Jack thought he was the only one that had changed around there, he realized he was wrong. The cars weren't actually the same, they were just new shitty old cars. Fifteen-year-old Jack was still at the Vagabond, it's just that he was now some fifteen-year-old named Chad or Jerry. Jack was the thirty-four-year-old homeless alcoholic guy that fifteen-year-old Jack had used to laugh at.

Nobody tore the buildings down, that much was true, but, just like people, they all entered the next sad phase of their existence and fulfilled their depressing purposes while eagerly awaiting a wrecking ball that never came. Even the ugly bitch who owned the Vagabond had changed. The old ugly bitch at the counter was actually the daughter of the owner who was the old ugly bitch who had always been at the manager's office when he was a teenager. Back then, the daughter had been in her early thirties. She had worked the grave shift after her mom's shift was over. Her perfect ass had always stretched the seams of a worn-in pair of Levi's, and her cleavage had always been half out of a low-cut t-shirt. Back then, Jack had been in love. Somewhere along the line, she had become her ugly old mom.

Jack couldn't see it in himself when he looked in the mirror in his room at the Vagabond; Jack still saw twenty-one-year-old Jack. He saw the Jack that girls had lined up to fix, but it was a fact that while a mirror might cast an accurate reflection of a person, an accurate reflection was not what a person looking in it perceived. It didn't matter if he could see it himself; he realized what other people saw, and he was all of a sudden envious of that old bitch's daughter. When he started to think about how he'd look at her age, she all of a sudden seemed a lot more vibrant and attractive than he'd given her credit for.

Jack's room at the Vagabond looked out over Pacific Highway to an ampm. A windfall of funds from a lucky encounter with a very careless heroin dealer had provided him the cash he was using to rent the room and buy the beer. He and another junkie hobo had rolled this particular heroin dealer when he was stupid enough to come down through City Hall Park after he'd been drinking at a downtown bar. Jack and his hobo partner had recognized the dealer right away. They had also recognized his intoxicated state. They both assumed he was holding, and their decision to roll him hadn't even been discussed, just acted on. They had been two predators closing on prey and instinct alone had guided their actions. Jack had picked up a club-sized downed branch and closed on the dealer. Within ten seconds, Jack had clubbed him like a baby seal, and his predator partner had grabbed the bag that dealer always had his stash in.

They split the stash, but Jack hadn't even stuck around the Yesler overpass for the rest of the night. Everybody under that overpass would know what

Jack was holding within an hour, and then he'd be the prey before morning came. He had walked south, past the stadiums. Down by the SoDo train tracks, he'd found a comfy little loading dock to catch some sleep in. He had gotten out his kit, lit up the spoon, drawn up a hit, and zonked out until morning. When he had woken up, he'd known he had to get out of Seattle for a while. He no longer knew anyone in Seattle to sell a significant stash of heroin to, not anyone he trusted. It had been a few years since he'd actually dealt drugs. He still had friends in Tacoma that he could safely unload the stash to, albeit at a discount of what it was worth. He had needed to sell it. If he hadn't sold it, he'd have shot it in a couple of days. Then he'd have been right back under the Yesler overpass chasing his next hit while simultaneously suffering withdrawal. He had been on a bus headed south before it was completely light out.

It seemed like a long walk to the ampm for another bottle of Night Train or a 40oz of Olde English 800. The walk seemed to get longer every few hours when the need for smokes or another bottle arose in him. He thought it might be because every trip down there might be the one where he didn't come back to the motel at all. Jack had been trying to work up the nerve to commit himself for days, but every time he got down to the payphone, he lost his nerve.

For some reason he wouldn't call from his room. Inside Room 311 everything seemed safe as long as the booze and smokes held out. There was a bed, a TV, and somewhere to piss and shit. It was also someplace to puke, something Jack was doing with more and more frequency on account of his liver being effectively shot and the heroin withdrawal he had been enduring. In his state, there was no longer any need for food. Jack managed his nutritional needs between microwave burritos at the ampm and the candy vending machine that was over by the icemaker at the Vagabond.

Every trip, he intended to make the call from the payphone. Most of the time, he got his backpack together and gathered any personal items he still planned on keeping and headed out the door toward the payphone, but every time he just ended up standing there in the store with a bottle in his hand. There was always a good excuse to put it off for another day, a few more hours, or for another bottle. Maybe there was a movie coming on that would make him nostalgic for other times. Since he used very little of the heroin before selling it, there was enough cash to survive at the Vagabond for a little while longer. Since he'd switched from heroin back to alcohol, he wouldn't run out of money buying more heroin. Drinking a few hundred dollars takes a lot longer than shooting it, and Jack needed that extra time to follow through on what he had come there to do. Sometimes he even lost his nerve before he left the room. If he didn't grab his backpack before he headed out, he knew he wasn't making the call that time. Those trips were actually better than the ones where he went through the whole dog and pony show of bringing his stuff with him. At least there were no expectations on him to follow through on those trips. The other times were harder.

One afternoon he got himself together in a hurry. He must have been thirsty the night before, because he'd drunk his eye-opener before he went to bed. After an entire day's sleep without any alcohol, he was in sad shape. Shaking all over, with a cigarette clinched between his lips, he started the walk toward the store. Regardless of whether he made the call this time or not, he'd still need that eye-opener just to get the shakes off him. It would be easy enough to grab a bottle, sit by the phone, and wait for the cops to show up. When they pulled up, he'd dust off the bottle and butt out his last smoke before they took them away from him, then off to the ward. He hadn't come to the Vagabond to commit himself, but at some point, Jack's plan to commit suicide had morphed into a last-ditch attempt to get back into Western State. He figured, if he played it right this time, he could stay there forever.

Walking down that row of rooms at the Vagabond always reminded him of walking down the wing of a single-floor prison. Shitty motels always reminded Jack a little bit of incarceration. The ones with second floors and covered walkways just reminded him of the types of prison wings with second floors and catwalks. They had the same type of layout, and they had the same type of desperation about them.

As he was crossing the street, he had that now-familiar feeling of being somewhere completely foreign despite coming out that way several times a day. Deterioration of his mind secondary to substance abuse could explain it. After all, with everything that had been done to Jack's mind by that point, it would be odd if anything ever seemed normal. But he figured it had more to do with the foreign nature of the action he was about to take. Jack had been committed many times, but he couldn't remember ever affirmatively requesting it, though maybe he had. His mind was so shot that he genuinely couldn't remember. It was the way an Alzheimer's patient or baby must have felt: complete unfamiliarity with the familiar.

Jack's heart was beating out of his chest at the proposition of getting himself committed. He then recognized that it was really going to happen that time. He was finally willing to go through with it.

For a few minutes, he stared across the street at his destination, at the payphone that he'd walked away from at least forty times over the last couple of weeks. Cars whizzed in front of him, occluding his view momentarily. "It was Tacoma, so of course they were old shitty economy models with no options, but when they passed, that payphone was there again." During a break in the traffic, he spit out his smoke and walked with a purpose toward it.

Chapter 18

Sometimes, Jack started off being very deliberate with the way he went about doing a thing because he needed it to seem perfect. Jack, of course, had OCD. Sometimes, though, he did it because he wanted to remember every detail of what he perceived to be a pivotal event in his life. Earlier had been one of those times. There he was, taking little mental snapshots of his own stride, flicking his smoke into the street, on his way to take back control of his life once and for all. He viewed it in his mind from a third-person perspective, like there was a camera crew filming him. It was all very dramatic. Sometime during that dramatic event, Jack's resolve faltered again. Then, he was right back in Room 311, sucking down beers and smoking cigarettes. It was later in the afternoon by that point. Jack's stomach was pretty upset, so he was drinking some weak Miller High Life. The malt liquor he normally drank was straight gut rot. The Mad Dog, Thunderbird, and Night Train were no better.

The next afternoon, Jack sat by that payphone for over an hour, and he took note of everything that happened. He decided to switch it up so he drank Wild Irish Rose and ate a hot dog while people came and went. No more than a handful ever bothered to notice him sitting on the curb. Over and over again, he told himself that he was just going to eat something to settle his stomach before making that three-digit phone call. For a while after that, he tried to keep track of the black ants that navigated the asphalt desert of the ampm parking lot. For about half an hour, it was an interesting glance into ant culture. Watching them pick up objects bigger than their own bodies and then set off for some unseen home base back in the bushes behind the phones somewhere was fascinating. They would dodge broken shards of glass, pebbles, and cigarette butts with a twig that weighed the equivalent of a fully-loaded pickup truck. All Jack could think was that if ants were humans, they would never have to go to the gym, and they'd still kick all the humans' asses. Thank God, he thought, ants weren't humans. But ants only seemed interesting until Jack needed more booze, and before he could even consider that he was supposed to be getting himself committed, he had another bottle in his hand and a smoke hanging out of his mouth. By the time he was halfway done with that bottle, he was too buzzed to go to Western

State, so he just grabbed an armload of Olde English 40oz's and two packs of Camels before going back to shitty Room 311.

A couple days after that, Jack hadn't made any further attempts to commit himself when he decided he'd head over to Todd's place for a visit. His cowardly behavior the other day was already scrubbed from his squeaky-clean mind. Alcohol had been a good cleanser for him, always had. It left everything spotless, even minds.

None of it really mattered right then, since, within a few days the money he'd gotten from the heroin would run out. When that happened, he'd be out of a room and out of money for booze. There was no other easy payday around the corner. That heroin dealer in City Hall Park was a gift and an aberration, nothing more. When the money from that dealer's heroin was gone, he'd either be back under an overpass or committed to Western State. Jack had had enough of the former; the latter needed to happen.

Something else was becoming an issue for Jack. By that time, it was getting harder and harder to keep his mind focused. Even when he wasn't drunk, he was confused all the time. One of those days, sitting by the payphone, he got up to get a bottle from the ampm, and when he came out, he found a full bottle sitting on the curb where he'd been sitting just a few minutes earlier. He'd just woken up, and wasn't even drunk, but he still had no recollection of buying the bottle. A few days before that, while he was buying a bottle, his total had come up on the cash register and he hadn't been able to make sense of the numbers. It was the same bottle he had bought a hundred times before, and the total was the same as it had always been, but he hadn't been able to make sense of the numbers on the cash register screen. It had been as though he'd never seen numbers before. Also, he hadn't been able to count the dollar bills in his wallet. He was stone-cold sober, it was first thing in the morning, and the cashier had needed to count Jack's money for him. "Well, it wasn't really first thing in the mornin,' more like my mornin,' which was like one thirty in the afternoon." A few days later, he had realized he couldn't read any of the words on a page in the newspaper. The confusion was bad enough, but by that time Jack also shook all over, whether he was drunk or not.

The day Jack went to visit Todd, he started walking to his house. He still liked walking, and it wasn't like he had anything he was going to be late for. Todd's apartment was pretty far, and it was raining pretty hard, but it always rained. Jack stopped at a bus stop after he'd walked about a mile nonetheless. It wasn't the rain—again, it rained all the time. He was afraid that if he walked all the way to Todd's he'd get too drunk on the way and black out.

Jack was soaked, and the bus was a greenhouse. That's what happened when you put twenty-five wet people in a metal box and turned the heat on. Instant greenhouse. Jack couldn't tell how much of the dampness he felt was rain or sweat. As he sat in the little hard plastic tandem bus seat, he hoped Todd's car was running so that he could give Jack a ride back to the motel. That was Jack's last trip anywhere before he took the big trip to Western State. He didn't have enough money to go anywhere else, and he was pretty sure he only had enough money for three more days of rent and booze.

Chapter 19

"Have I mentioned that I'd been having a hard time keepin' my mind focused around that time? Well, I had, and it was fuckin' infuriatin.' Back then, I considered findin' some hyperactive kid and stealin' his Ritalin."

Jack's visit with Todd didn't happen. During the last few years, Todd had let Jack crash at his place often and given him money here and there. He could have lived there, and Todd had offered, but at that juncture Jack preferred to only impose on Todd when he was really hard up. At that point in life, Jack chose to self-destruct on his own. Todd never expected to be paid back, and, as always, he held onto Jack's record collection for him.

When Jack finally got off the bus at Todd's place, it didn't look right. His car was gone. That was strange, because, even if his car was running, Todd never left home for more than an hour at a time, mostly just to get weed, cigarettes, and food. When Jack got up to Todd's apartment, he could see in through the window. Everything was different. Jack didn't know who lived there, but based on the décor, he knew it wasn't Todd's place anymore.

It turned out some girl lived there now. She started beating on the window and threatening to call 911 when she saw Jack peering through her window. For a minute Jack had some hope that she was just some girl that had moved in with Todd, but when he inquired, she just yelled "This is my apartment. I don't know any Todd."

It shouldn't have surprised him. People moved, and Jack had been in the wind for a long time. He could have found Todd if he'd looked around a little. He could have called the last phone number he had for Ron. For that matter, he could have called the last number he had for Todd. He could have called Todd's number from his motel room before he went over there in the first place, but he had just wanted to show up. Todd may have moved, but he had probably kept his phone number. Todd had moved before, but he'd always kept that same number. If he'd looked, he could have found Todd. If he'd looked, he could have found any of them, Beth, Ron, even his brother Laurence. He just didn't want to anymore. It was still raining, but it had let up a bit. He decided to walk back to the Vagabond, and by that time it really didn't matter if he blacked out on the way, so he stopped and got a bottle of

Thunderbird.

Right then, he knew he wasn't even really trying to find Todd that day at all. If he had been, he would have found him. It was just the last of the last excuses he could indulge before the inevitable. There was a payphone in an ampm parking lot waiting for him to make a three-digit phone call, and he'd avoided it long enough.

Chapter 20

I f there was one thing Jack had an abundance of in his life, it was time to ponder his situation and reflect on his actions. Not that it had given him any insight into himself. None that had helped him to understand or navigate the world any better, anyway. Whether it was time well-spent on someone that reflected and made adjustments to better meet life on life's terms, or time completely wasted on someone that would never understand how to get by, it was time that existed. Jack couldn't do shit with it. He never could, and he would never be able to. It was a flaw. He had a thousand of them, but Jack was actually a pretty lovable guy. How could someone be so fatalistically miserable but also be the person that you had the best time with? How could someone be so fucked up, but seem so close to savable. Who knows, but it was true. How it was true is simply a question without an answer.

Jack was a Thorazine zombie after that. He routinely took comfort in that fact that he wasn't a drooler or wall walker, just a garden variety Thorazine zombie. Since everyone was on Thorazine at Western State, he never gave it a designation like the other groups around there, the Cliff Claven, droolers, etc. He'd also never been as snowed as he was at Western State that time.They kept him zombified twenty-four hours a day. Those poor wall walkers and droolers didn't have a sense of themselves left. Even pumped full of Thorazine, Jack still periodically remembered himself, who he was, what he was about. For better or worse, there was still some Jack left inside Jack's skull, but not much. Those poor wall walkers and droolers, their foreheads might as well have had neon signs affixed to them, flashing the word "VACANT." "Shit, you could nail the fuckin' signs to those fuckers' foreheads. They wouldn't even know the difference. No-fuckin'-body home! Trust me when I fuckin' tell you that."

After he settled in, he started spending most of his time just roaming around the ward. That is, he would roam when he wasn't too comatose to get out of bed. There was no way to tell how many hours of the day he spent in bed wide awake but too doped up to realize he was conscious. When his head was clear enough to think about it, mostly while he was roaming around, he figured it was a lot of the hours of the day. If he were being honest with himself, he'd have said most of the hours of the day were likely spent in that state. For Jack, the number of hours of the day where he was able to form these somewhat coherent thoughts and inquiries was pretty limited. The remainder of his thoughts were distorted and bizarre. He figured he'd been at Western State for several months. It was sunny outside, and inside his ward it was unbearably hot every day. When he got there, it was definitely cold and wet every day. When he wasn't comatose, he had an extremely restless feeling emanating from inside him. It forced him to roam constantly. He had been sure the feeling was a side effect of one of the medications he was on. He wondered why Beth wasn't there too, but during those hours he mostly roamed.

Chapter 21

J ack was fading into the mosaic of that place fast. Then, one day, he wasn't. One day, he was in a warm bed in a small two-bedroom house in the Hawthorne District of Portland Oregon. There was money on the table in the kitchen, so he took it and walked to the Plaid Pantry and got some Tim's Cascade Jalapeño potato chips and a Coke. It all seemed very normal and familiar, but he had no idea why. He knew his way there, and he knew his way back to the house he'd woken up in. It felt like a routine, even though he couldn't remember doing it before. He went back to the house where he'd woken up. He went inside and turned on the TV. The news was on, and it was about a war in Iraq or Afghanistan. Both? Jack wasn't really listening, but he couldn't have told you where the war was even if he had been, but probably Iraq or Afghanistan. A car pulled up in the driveway. A minute later, Beth walked in wearing turquoise scrubs.

She'd been in Portland for a about six years. She

was an RN working in the ER at OHSU Hospital now. Her old boss at Western State had called her when she saw Jack was a patient on one of the wards. Beth had spent several months and a great deal of time and money arranging for Jack to be released to her care, which he ultimately was.

Jack had actually been living with her for about two years. Sometimes he knew that. Sometimes he didn't. Sometimes he knew that he lived there with Beth but didn't know for how long. Sometimes he knew everything and was pretty normal. Those were the days when they'd go for a drive and have a picnic.

Beth deserved something better, and she could have had it. She wouldn't have taken it, though. She wouldn't have taken that something better if it had been delivered to her door wrapped in a million dollars. Her something better was Jack. Most people would agree that her something better was something much worse, but she would've spent every cent in the world to get it. Getting him there did cost her nearly every cent she had in the world, but he was there. They were both there. That was all.

Afterword

I can't say where you came across this book, but my best guess would be that you found it in a box of castoff garbage by the curb outside the cheap apartment complex at the end of your road. That guy that lived in the noisy apartment was just evicted, and this little novella was just some superfluous stack of somewhat uninformative paper disguised as a book by a cheap book binding and publishing house logo. Trust me, even the publishing house logo is a smoke show, just my plausible camouflage for a self-publishing operation consisting of me, and me alone, a one-man band.

As you might have already guessed from the title, this is the third part of a story. It's also the end of Jack's story. Jack is a guy that consistently failed to clear a bar so low he could have tripped over it. Jacks are all over the world. Most of you know a Jack. I've known several. I've even been a Jack in the past. I spend a lot of time and effort these days doing my best not to turn back into a Jack, but I digress. That noisy guy from the recently vacated apartment is definitely a Jack. He's not a bad guy. He's actually a pretty fun guy under the right set of circumstances. Anyway, there are two more novellas, and Jack has got a lot more story to tell.

If you are missing one or both of the other novellas, keep digin' through enough dumpsters, you might find them. If not, the novellas have been combined into one volume, *The Complete Down and Out in Seattle and Tacoma Series*, I saw one the other day on the free book rack outside the Powell's in downtown Portland. I guess the entire series is Courting Mediocrity!

About the Author

I was a homeless teenager. Now I own a home. I was a high school dropout. Now I'm an attorney. I was an alcoholic. Now I'm sober. I was a kid well into adulthood. Now I'm the adult parent of kids. I was alone. Now I have people. I was a punk rock teenager. Now I'm a punk rock middleager. I was Jack. Now I'm Chris.

Thank you for reading Squatting in the Shadow of an Ant. I hope you enjoyed it. Reviews are the single most important factor to the success or failure of a book. Please take a moment and leave a short review at one, or preferably both of the links below. Also please connect with me on social media, and join my email list for freebies.

Connect with Me and Subscribe to the Email List

https://blandcoffeepublishing.com

Also by Christopher J. Stockwell

If you love slummin' it in the PNW, check out the rest of the down and out series. If you don't feel icky afterward, we'll refund your money.

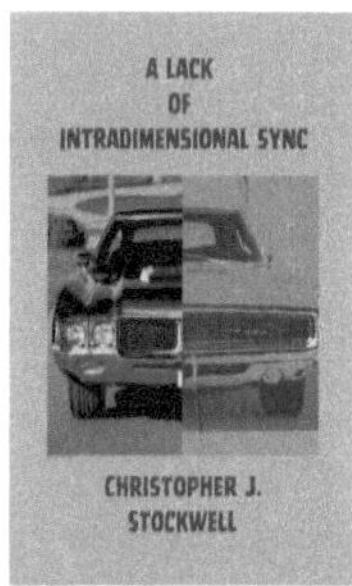

A Lack of Intradimensional Sync

Jon is everywhere an nowhere. He slips out of himself and rides the infinite roads of existence itself. But infinite time is eventually infinite torment for a human brain that never asked for anything more than normality. Expected Release 2026.

Sleeping in the Daytime: Novella One

The keystone of the down and out books, a first glance at Jack. He's the car wreck you can't take your eyes off. Sleeping in the Daytime lets you see him before serious deterioration has set in. Get ready, living like Jack is a full-time job.

Courting Mediocrity: Novella Two

See what's next for Jack. Quiet anonymity in a boring town or city or whatever isn't his style.

The Complete Down and Out in Seattle and Tacoma Series

The three novellas of the Down and Out in Seattle and Tacoma Series in one volume. The down and out novellas are like coke, alcohol, and cigarettes. You can enjoy them separately, but they were meant to be consumed together.

City Attorney's Office: Book One, ProfessionalCamouflage

This first of a series of short romance novels is nothing more than a thinly-veiled disguise for a social and political satire piece. Is is dark humor, literary existential bullshit, a boring workplace romance. I don't fuckin' know, and I wrote the book.

City Attorney's Office Book Two: The Land of Lollipops and Suckers

This second, and last (?) of the City Attorney's Office books. People always ask me if a lawyer's life is like Law & Order or the Good Wife. It's neither, it's mostly like Matlock and Perry Mason having a beer with Saul Goodman. Enjoy!

The Complete City Attorney's Office Series

If you liked the love triangle between Ben, Maria, and Erin, you'll get closure. If you liked that fact that Ben is a monkey wrench dismantling the necessary cogs of justice, it's in there as well. If you just want the series to be over, so do it. Your welcome!

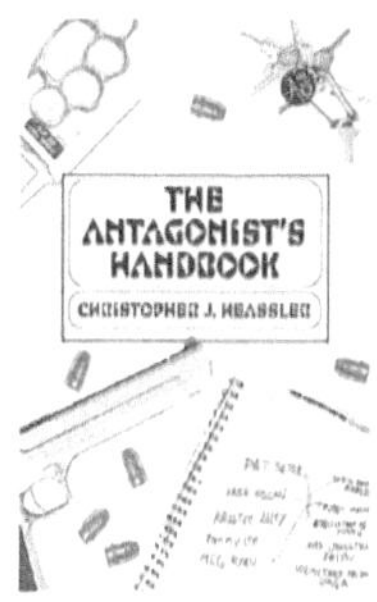

The Antagonist's Handbook

Stockwell's first novel, written under the pseudonym Christopher J. Heassler details the emergence of a paparazzi gang who exploit celebrities. The Antagonist's Handbook has long been out of print, but is scheduled for re-release in 2026.